SAVAGE SECRETS

MAFIA ELITE, BOOK 4

AMY MCKINLEY

ARROWSCOPE PRESS, LLC

THE FAMILY

Chicago Outfit
Italian American Mafia

Caruso Family
Maximus "Max" (son, boss, married Liliana Brambilla)
Elena (adopted daughter)
Tony (son)
Parents/former boss
Antonio – (father, former boss, deceased)
Maria (first wife to Antonio, deceased, Max's Mom)
Nicole (second wife to Antonio (Tony's Mom, Elena's adopted Mom))
Vito (advisor to boss)
Maria's family from Italy
Salvio "Sal" (cousin)
Cristiano (cousin)
Tommasso (cousin)
Aunt Rosa (lives in Sicily)

<u>Brambilla Family</u>
Liliana "Lil" (daughter – married Max Caruso)
Leonardo (underboss, cousin)
Dino (advisor to boss)
Eva (cousin, deceased)
Parents/former boss
Benito (former boss, deceased)
Julia (Benito's wife, deceased)
Vincenzo (Julia's Sicilian father, Liliana's grandfather)

<u>La Rosa Family</u>
Marco (son, boss)
Nico (son)
Trey (son)
Sofia (daughter, married Enzo Vitale)
Maso (Robert's brother, advisor)
Tom (captain)
Parents/former boss
Robert (former boss)
Angela (Robert's wife)

<u>Vitale Family</u>
Enzo (son, boss, married Sofia La Rosa)
Emiliana "Em" (daughter, married Stefano Rossi)
Aldo (advisor to boss)
Renato "Ren" (captain)
Parents/former boss
Emilio (former boss)
Alessia (Emilio's wife)

<u>Rossi Family</u>
Stefano (son, boss, capo dei capi (boss of all bosses), married
Emiliana Vitale)
Camila (daughter, married Vic Pavlov)

Alfonso (son, deceased)
Marissa (daughter, deceased)
Drago (advisor to the boss)
Parents/former boss
Frank (father, former boss, deceased)
Carla (Frank's wife, deceased)

Russian Mafia
Pavlov Bratva

Pavlov Bratva
Yuri (boss)
Mischa (wife)
Ivan (eldest son, former underboss, deceased)
Victor "Vic" (son, underboss, married Camila Rossi)
Katya (angel of death, assassin)

CHAPTER ONE

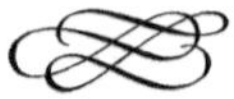

ELENA

I ran as if the hounds of hell were on my heels. My enemies, the Russians or perhaps the Italians, were coming for me. I wasn't positive which faction would hunt me first. The Bratva, the Russian Mafia, was a sure thing and always a threat, whereas the Chicago arm of the Italian Mafia's intentions were unknown. I'd lived among one of the ruling Five Families for most of my life. I was one of them.

After my mother, Daniela —a distant cousin of one of the Italian families—was murdered, Nicole Caruso pressured her husband to adopt me. She'd wanted a daughter. That very day, I became Elena Caruso, something I never regretted as I assumed the role of Mafia princess. She'd taught many things, taking over where my mother had left off. One of the most important was how to change my appearance, to be a chameleon.

A horn blared as a car passed in front of me, and my surroundings snapped back into focus. Chilly fall air gusted off the Hudson River as I crossed the street from my studio in Maxwell Place. A shiver raced along my spine.

I'd been uneasy since five o'clock that morning, when the shrill sound of my alarm shocked me awake. I'd rushed through getting ready, laced up my gym shoes, and hit the pavement not even ten minutes later. A heavy dose of dread had settled on my shoulders, increasing in weight with each minute that passed.

My mind was chaotic, making it difficult to enjoy the beauty of running along the walkway with markets and trendy shops on my left and the river on my right. The area would bustle with activity soon, as festivals and fairs were a constant during the fall in the popular North End of Hoboken, New Jersey. I loved that about the location, but the ominous vibe I carried with me made it hard to enjoy.

The influx of people so near to where I lived only increased my sense of trepidation. Triggered by an elusive ghost that haunted my dreams, I let my mind wander to the skills my birth mother had taught me—how to create a disguise through hair, makeup, and carriage. I'd used those lessons from the onset of detection by the Bratva, the day my mother was killed and Nicole saved me.

I had cut my unusual dual shade of warm-brunette and caramel hair so that the ends brushed the tops of my shoulders instead falling in waves down my back. I'd dyed it black, and brown contacts hid my light eyes. My natural blue-green color had gotten me into trouble more than once, and I needed to blend, fade into the crowd, and become unnoticed—forgettable.

The makeup I wore was to help me look older, not to enhance any particular feature. My hair was a drab black, not shiny and healthy. As for clothes, the baggier, the better. Even the jewelry I chose was costume, the style so far from what I normally would have worn. Put everything together, and I was just another person in a crowd. Nothing about me was memorable, which was exactly how I wanted it.

But underneath my sloppy attire, my body was toned and strong. I increased my pace, weaving around fellow joggers, my earbuds keeping the pretense that music pumped through them. It didn't. That would have been a rookie mistake. I needed every sense on alert when I was in public. The ripple of the water I ran adjacent to and the strenuous rhythmic motion of running both helped to calm the itchy sensation of my enemies closing in on me. Only two people knew that I was alive, and they would never tell. I was safe. It'd been four years. There was no reason things would change.

With each mile that dissolved under the relentless pounding of my feet, the tension eased, and I was able to push aside the waking paranoia and enjoy the run. Bricks paved the walkway, and a wrought iron railing separated the people walking and running from the river along the tree-lined expanse. Not far across the water, New York's skyline reached for the clouds, complete with a view of Lady Liberty.

Hoboken itself was vibrant and packed with cafes, bars, and shops, and I had easy access to New York with several modes of transportation, but my favorite was hopping the ferry that took me to Manhattan, where I worked during the day at a bookstore. If possible, I tried to work the morning shift—there weren't as many customers—but today had landed me an afternoon slot. At least I could grab a coffee and pastry from the café in my building after showering. It was something to look forward to.

In the four years that I'd lived there, I'd kept to myself. I had acquaintances but no close friends other than Danny, whom I'd met in college, but that was more of a working relationship. Granted, it doubled as a way to keep my skills in top shape and gave me an adrenaline high in the very uneventful life I'd been leading, as I helped him some nights to find blind spots in the security systems he designed for commercial and residential properties. He was a hacker and had access to security feeds, and we were a good team. People knew me as Chloe James, and aside from having classes together here or there, no one had any information about me. It was better that way.

A peek at my black running watch told me I was at the

halfway point of the distance I wanted to cover. I glanced over my shoulder to ensure no one was close then turned around to head back as my phone, strapped to my bicep, buzzed. It wasn't the first time that'd happened so early in the morning, as the sun was just cresting the horizon. Many times, my manager would call incessantly, knowing I was usually free, as he scrambled to rearrange the schedule when someone called off an early shift.

It looked like I would have to take that coffee and pastry with me onto the ferry. I increased my pace to get home sooner and return the call. Not that I couldn't do so there, but no one else would agree to come in early, so there was no rush for me to respond until I finished my run.

Soon, I was sprinting. A few more missed calls came across from the vibrations along my arm, and I grinned at his persistence. As I neared Maxwell Place, I slowed my pace so I could cool down. I would have to forgo stretching until I got upstairs and returned the call.

When the crosswalk signal changed to allow pedestrians to go, I hurried to the other side then made my way into the building. The studio was paid for in full by a bank account owned under the guise of Chloe James's mother, Rachel James. Chloe was the benefactor and co-owner. It was another layer to deter detection.

The elevator ride to the fourth floor was quick, and as soon as I was in my apartment, I undid the Velcro securing my phone to my arm. Slipping it from the clear plastic sleeve, I glanced at the screen, expecting to see missed calls from my manger. But instead, my phone lit up with several calls from Sofia, the only person from my old life who knew my number or where I was. That alone was disconcerting. But my blood froze at a text from Katya: *If I can find you, they can. It's time to go home.*

I tightened my grip on the phone and warily glanced around the apartment. I could hear the blood pumping in my ears as I strained for the sound of a floorboard creaking. I took in every detail of the space before me, which was a mixture of wide-plank hardwood floors, stone, and brushed metal. Oversized windows framed the Hudson River and New York skyline. I swept over every detail, checking for the slightest thing out of place, but it was as I'd left it, complete with the blue-gray throw hung in a haphazard mess across the back of the couch and my glass of water on the quartz island.

I lurched forward, the coffee table a couple of feet away. In a hidden compartment on the rear of the table were my escape bag and weapons. I traced the bottom of the wood until I felt the trigger pop the cabinet open.

As soon as the door swung wide, I swiped my bag and palmed the 9mm. My heart beat against my ribs in a furious tempo, and the heightened awareness of the ticking clock bit at my heels as I tore my running clothes off then replaced them with a pair of jeans, a long-sleeved black shirt, and a nondescript black hoodie. I slipped on black gym shoes then tied them securely. In my emergency backpack, I kept a change of clothes, more ammo, money, a water bottle, a dishwater-blond wig, a first aid kit, and most importantly, IDs with a different identity.

I slung the backpack on and tightened the straps before sliding the gun into the waistband of my jeans. I pulled the hem of the hoodie down to cover it then rushed to the front door. I would miss the place, especially the private rooftop terrace, where I'd spent many evenings reading or studying. It was a luxury I hadn't been able to resist.

I grabbed the doorknob, and I yanked it open, ready to sprint to the stairs—only I couldn't. I was too late. I nearly slammed into a man with dark hair, eyes as green as a lawn in the springtime, and a body that promised hours of sin. Marco La Rosa, the most infuriating man I'd ever met, had found me.

He stood, all six foot two inches of him, blocking my way with wide shoulders that filled the doorframe—and I wasted precious seconds taking him in. Sofia's oldest brother, boss of the La Rosa family, was probably the reason why she'd called repeatedly. He was terrifyingly beautiful, fierce, loyal, and from what I'd been told, a total man-whore. All I cared about, though, was escape and where his loyalties lay.

The absolute deadly stillness that surrounded him triggered my reactions, and I used all my strength to slam the door.

He stopped it then pushed it wide and stepped across the threshold and into my space. "Found you, little thief."

CHAPTER TWO

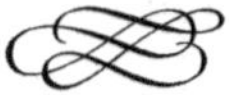

ELENA

ittle thief. The childhood nickname Marco resurrected hit me at the same time as the thud of his hand stopping the door from closing in his face. It was a name that had become a reality once I'd gone into hiding. I had a set of skills that Danny utilized often, last night's handful of hours of sleep a physical reminder of my silent partnership in his security company, where I broke into new clients' properties to test the validity of what he'd designed. But it wasn't the time to dwell on the irony of what Marco had called me or that my involvement in Danny's business had just reached an end.

There was nowhere to run. The only way out was to fight. I'd faced off with Marco before. He always won, but not this time. I needed to best him then get the hell away, fast. I was glad that I'd tightened the straps on my backpack when I put it on— it would need to be secure when my chance to slip past him presented itself.

"I don't know what you're talking about." It was pointless, but I had to try. I did look different with my colored contacts, shorn and dyed hair, and nondescript clothes. "Who is it you're looking for?"

The side of his mouth curved into that damn crooked grin of his, the one that made my knees weak but also signaled trouble. My fingers tightened around the keys to my place as he stepped closer, and I swore the space shrank with his larger-than-life presence filling it. We never got along when we were teenagers, each of us provoking the other time and again. All the calls must have been Sofia trying to warn me. She knew the animosity between her oldest brother and me. *Why him? Couldn't Sofia, or anyone else in the Five Families, have come to get me?*

"Going somewhere?" He ignored my question, his eyebrow quirking up. Sarcastic bastard. "Chloe James? Don't think for one second I don't know you're Elena. I'd recognize you anywhere, in any disguise." He ran a forefinger along the side of my neck. "This freckle, the shape of your eyes, the pout of your lips, even the smell of your skin. You can't hide from me. It doesn't matter what alias you use. I'll always find you."

"Really?" I mirrored his cocky expression with a raised brow of my own. "Took you long enough."

His head tipped back, and as rich laughter spilled from his lips, I shivered from his wicked masculinity. Beneath the feigned hate, I was more than attracted to him. But it wasn't a mask on his part. He'd never trusted me and had made sure I knew we were enemies almost from the start.

I inched to the right, intent on getting him away from the door. His green eyes sparkled with mirth and a hint of mischief that I was more than familiar with as he crowded me. That close, his knee-weakening, warm, woody scent tempted me to lean into him, but I feigned indifference by grimacing—self-preservation at its strongest. We were sworn enemies from our teen years, and there was no way I would let him know the truth of my traitorous heart.

"Why are you here, Marco?" I held still, waiting for an opportunity to make my move and dart past him. "I've been gone for four years. Why now?"

"You mean why me and not your brother?"

"That's not what I meant, and you know it." Tony was sort of my brother. I was adopted. He wasn't. Even though we grew up together, we weren't close at all. I wouldn't have expected him to take the slightest interest in my welfare, as he never had before.

"I'm here because it's dangerous, and your location is compromised." His gaze darted around my condo, and I subtly adjusted my weight to the balls of my feet. "You never should have left."

It's now or never. I executed a front-thrust kick to his abdomen, hoping to stun him or knock him back enough to run. His damn reflexes were instant, and he avoided my leg. I moved forward, following through with a punch. His forearm blocked it, and my keys flew from my hand. He'd shifted another step away from the door, that evil grin back in place. With my keys out of my grasp, he thought he had me. He was wrong. I dashed into the hallway, knowing he would be on me in two seconds flat. But I had to try.

"Just like old times, huh, Elena?"

I fled down the hall, slammed into the steel door to the stairs, then burst through it as his taunting words followed. My feet barely touched the steps as I hurtled toward the landing. The sound of the door opening then closing caused the fine hairs on the back of my neck to rise in awareness of his pursuit. I'd been training to outrun, outshoot, and fight whoever came for me first. With Marco, running was my best option.

I pushed through to the lobby on the ground floor then pivoted to the rear entrance rather than the closer front doors. I hoped he didn't know about the back, where the employees came in, and that it would give me a small enough head start. At that time of day, there was a smaller chance of running into anyone, as most of the condo's staff were in their offices or doing whatever needed doing. Still, it was as if he was breathing down my neck. I didn't dare turn around to see how close he was or if he even followed me.

The contents of my backpack, probably the extra gun, thudded against my spine with each step. I would rearrange it when there was enough distance between us and I had a chance to breathe.

I slammed my hands against the release bar for the heavy steel door that led to the back alley. Cold air slapped me in the face, cooling my heated cheeks. The unpleasant smell of garbage from the dumpsters permeated the area. My toes dug into the pavement for purchase, and I took off at a sprint. The end of the block wasn't far ahead. Small pebbles ground against the asphalt beneath my feet, and I pumped my arms, lengthening my stride to quicken my pace.

It was wiser to stay in the alleys, at least for the time being. While I could lose myself in the crowds, the sidewalk was a little too congested and close to Maxwell Place for my taste. I neared the end of the alley, and my spine tingled. He was in pursuit. I knew it without having to look over my shoulder.

I sprinted to the end of the alley and almost had to skid to a stop. The crowd was thick with morning rush hour traffic, probably headed to New York City. I weaved through pedestrians as fast as I could, trying not to cause a commotion. Ducking behind a rather robust man, I flipped my hood up, concealing my head. If I didn't do something quickly, Marco would be on me. I could practically feel his large, calloused hand curling around my arm. Good thing almost all of my skin was covered and I wouldn't have to feel his touch, however much I might have liked it. Scowling, I adjusted my thoughts. I wouldn't enjoy it—he was a potential enemy.

Quickening my pace, I dodged into a familiar breakfast café and headed toward the rear door. I'd scoped out several places early on, in case I needed a fast escape. The muscles in my thighs were starting to cramp from pushing myself so hard on my morning run then fleeing from Marco. At this point, adrenaline was my friend. I would overcome anything to be free. I had no idea what Marco's intentions were, not really, especially after that wicked expression of his before I bolted.

The jingle of the bell sounded as I opened the door wide enough to squeeze through. It was packed with waiting customers, and the hostess tried to stop me as I mumbled about meeting friends. Heading toward the back with her distracted by the sound of the door, I kept my gaze focused on the escape mere feet away. *Please don't let that be Marco who entered behind me.*

I wanted to believe it wasn't him, but the flash of awareness that crawled all over my body told me otherwise. What I didn't understand was why he hadn't caught me already. I was fast, but I knew firsthand that he was faster, unless time had slowed him down. One could hope.

At the restaurant's back, I passed the restrooms then made a sharp turn toward the kitchen. The heavenly smells of bacon, eggs, and pancakes teased me but didn't slow my pace. Cries rose over my presence from the cooks and a waitress picking up her order. It didn't matter. I was almost to the door. I leapt over a box not yet put away from a recent delivery then slammed into the rear exit. My bodyweight propelled the door open.

I dug my toes into the asphalt, pivoted, then sprinted down the alleyway that was unfortunately not too far from where I lived. Midway down, a figure stepped from behind a dumpster, and I froze.

The early morning sun glinted off his gun—the one pointed directly at my head.

CHAPTER THREE

ELENA

I skidded to a halt and reached for the Glock secured in my waistband, desperate to shoot the hit man, who stood mere feet from me with a gun trained on my head, before he ended my life. A small part of me realized I should already have been dead.

Tall, lean, and with dark hair and eyes, he leered at me. I didn't recognize him. Before my hand could curl around my gun, he fired a shot at my feet.

"Elena Caruso?" He growled with a heavy Russian accent, and I knew his inquiry into my identity was the reason for the hesitation. I looked different enough. It would help for only so long before he matched my bone structure and features to how I used to look.

My pulse kicked up to an unhealthy rhythm as fear crawled through my veins. They'd found me. The Bratva had been after me since I was young but had thought I'd died when Antonio Caruso did. A little over four years ago, I'd gotten word they knew I was alive—that was why I had to go on the run, aided by Sofia and Katya, the Bratva's assassin.

I schooled my features enough to mask all thoughts except feigned confusion. My brows furrowed. "No. My name's Chloe."

"Hands where I see them." The hit man ushered me closer with his gun. Fine by me. The less space between us, the better chance I had at defending myself. In the distance, the sound of a door opening registered in the back of my mind. "Ah, I see it now. Same eyes and the shape of your face—it is you, little Elena. Perhaps we'll have a little fun before I kill you, hm?"

The evil curve of his lips pierced my heart at the same time his gun drilled a bullet into my leg. I felt the impact seconds before the burn of the wound and immediately shifted my weight away. Warmth oozed down my thigh, contrasting the chilly air, as shocks of pain zinged up and down my leg. I was going to have to make a grab for my gun and hope that he hesitated before ending my life. I knew whoever put the hit out on me wanted me dead—I had the scar from when I was young to prove it.

As he fumbled with his phone and what looked like a text message, I saw my chance and lowered my hands, inching my right one toward the gun hidden behind my back.

A door closed loudly, and the hit man jerked his gaze up just as a bullet too close for comfort burned past my head to *thunk* into the center of his forehead. I stood frozen as the hit man's head jerked from the impact where a small hole formed. As if in slow motion, his body crumpled to the ground. Still, I didn't move.

Another surge of adrenaline flooded my body, fueling me to keep moving. I didn't know Marco's intentions, at least not after so much time had passed since I last saw him. I took a shaky step forward, and white-hot pain splintered along my thigh before I lurched to the side as my leg gave out. Bracing myself to slam into the asphalt, I squeezed my eyes shut and put my hands out to brace my fall. Only I never hit the ground. Strong arms encircled me, and I felt myself lifted off my feet and cradled against a solid chest. I cracked my eyelids open and curled my hands into the black Henley stretched across Marco's impressive shoulders.

What the hell am I going to do now?

<hr>

Marco

The moment I pushed through the doorway and into the alley, the horror of the scene branded my mind. I could lose her—*again*. A gunshot echoed off the buildings on either side, and Elena buckled. She shifted to her uninjured leg as my world tunneled to the threat in front of her.

Why he hadn't fired a kill shot was a mystery, but I wasn't going to look that gift horse in the mouth.

He was in my sight. I prayed Elena wouldn't move as I squeezed the trigger of my 9mm. There was no hesitation. When the bullet struck the center of the assassin's forehead, I took my first full breath after stepping through that door and into a nightmare.

It would have been better if the guy's death looked like a mugging. I jogged up to Elena and clasped her elbow. "Hold on a second. Then I'll get you out of here."

Her jaw locked tight, but she managed a nod. When I was sure she wouldn't try to run again, I bent to her attacker, riffled through his pockets, and pulled out his wallet. Next, I picked up his phone, scanning the text that was cued to send. He'd been calling in the kill order through text but hadn't sent it. I hit Send, hoping to buy us more time. I memorized the number attached to the text then threw the phone and the gun in a nearby dumpster. I hauled the dead weight of him up and launched him in next. The billfold went into my pocket to go through later.

"Give me your belt." Her voice was strong, even laced with pain.

I was already unbuckling it, sliding it through the loops. When it was free, I knocked her hand away and bent to secure it in tourniquet fashion around her upper thigh to slow the bleeding. Then I lifted her into my arms.

There was no protest. She had to have been in a lot of pain not to fight me.

"We need to get somewhere secure, and I'll take care of this for you." I was staying in Manhattan, which would do us no good. After she rested for a while, when we found a safe enough room, we would head to my hotel.

"There's a first aid kit in my backpack." She lay her cheek against my chest, and I held her tighter. Elena had always infuriated me, no matter how obsessed I was with her. I'd never acted on it. She wasn't mine, and I'd known that from a young age. The problem was, I wasn't sure whose she was, and that wasn't referencing the marriage contract between her and Enzo, who was now my brother-in-law.

We had to leave the alleyway and reenter pedestrian traffic on the sidewalk. Her wound wasn't visible, as I'd picked her up so that it was against my chest. Not the most comfortable for her, but I knew she understood. I didn't like how much blood she was losing and needed to find the closest place to patch her up.

"There's a hotel a block over." Her voice was muffled and any rigidity she'd maintained in her posture was gone.

I had to hurry. As the morning lengthened, more people crowded the sidewalks on their way to work. I kept an eye out for any threats. After a couple of minutes, we were in front of the hotel she'd referenced. I used my back to push through the revolving door then bypassed the reception desk for the elevators. Elena didn't question me.

We rode the elevator in silence. "Hang on to me." As her

arms went around my neck, I shifted her enough to reach the dead guy's wallet—I would use his money. I set it on her stomach then secured her in my embrace again. "Pull out whatever cash is in there." When she slipped out a wad of hundreds —thankfully, it was US currency—I flagged down one of the maids cleaning a room. As she exited the room and was midstep to push her cart to the next, she spotted us.

"We need the room for a few hours." Elena didn't need any prodding and extended her arm to the maid with what had to be a couple thousand dollars. "And we were never here."

The maid's eyes went wide as she took the money then quickly stuffed it into the pocket of her uniform. She turned and opened the door to the room she'd cleaned, fixed a *do not disturb* sign to the doorknob, then held it open for us.

Once we were inside the modern room decorated in gray and silver with a king-sized bed, I secured the door behind us then carried Elena into the bathroom and set her in the bathtub. I needed to get a good look at her leg. She slipped out of the straps of her backpack then reclined so that she rested against the back of the tub.

After unzipping her bag, I located the kit she'd mentioned and pulled out scissors. I cut her jeans away from just above the injury then peeled the fabric down her leg. There was a lot of blood, but it wasn't pumping in time with her heart, indicating that the bullet hadn't hit a major artery.

Seeing her that way made too many emotions war through me. Anger won. "What the hell were you thinking?" I growled as I doused the gunshot wound with alcohol. She hissed but said nothing.

Instead of fighting with her, I clamped my teeth together until pain radiated along my jaw. The bullet had gone through her leg. I had to clean it, glue it closed, get her some fluids, and let her rest. I got to work, and Elena's head fell back against the tiles as she stopped keeping track of everything I was doing, obviously working on not passing out from the pain. That wound had to have hurt.

I handed her water from her pack then washed my hands and grabbed the towels stacked on a shelf in the bathroom. It was a good thing she was in there with me—I couldn't leave her alone for too long. She was resourceful and could easily disappear. As my hands curled around the soft white towels, I needed a second to gather my thoughts.

This is a shit show. We didn't know why the Russians were after her, only that they'd killed her mother. But the Bratva underboss, Ivan Pavlov's, single-minded determination led me to believe there was more to his hunt. Once the Bratva had a target, it wasn't uncommon for them to wipe out the entire line. Women and children were not exempt.

Italians rarely murdered women, and we did everything possible to rehome the children. Nicole and Antonio Caruso followed Italian tradition. After the Bratva killed Elena's mother, they saved her.

I shoved away from the sink, towels in hand. The steady rise and fall of Elena's chest gave me a modicum of comfort, but her beautiful face was void of color, making the long lashes that rested on her cheeks stand out even more. I tossed the bath mat onto the floor as I sat next to her. Blood seeped from the circular wound, coating the bottom of the tub beneath her.

The kit she had held everything I needed to take care of her, and there were pain pills, too, which I gave her two of to help dull the agony of the wound. We had to keep moving. Staying there was too dangerous. I had to get my stuff from the hotel then get us on the jet for home, but she needed a little time before we went on the run once more.

I removed her shoes and socks then cleaned the injury and a good portion of her leg to ward off infection before applying surgical glue. I held her severed skin together, giving the glue time to adhere. With care, I rolled her to her side to address the exit wound, noting how she flinched. I paused. "Are you okay?"

"Yes." She clenched her teeth. "Just finish, please."

I nodded, trying to work as quickly and gently as I could. After the glue seemed like it would hold, I covered the area with a bandage. I wasn't ready to sever contact, and my touch lingered. My hand rested on her hip, and I waited for her to pass out or say something. I was comfortable enough with our location to give her an hour or two before we had to move.

While her eyes were closed, I studied her. Even though I couldn't see them and the brown contacts covered her actual color, her eyes were stunning kaleidoscopes that had fascinated me as a kid—and an adult. Her ocean eyes were an intoxicating mixture of blues and greens and specks of gold.

The way she wore her hair, cut so that it brushed the top of her shoulders, was sleek and sophisticated, but I missed the thick caramel waves that fell down her back, with softer strands near her face, accentuating her high cheekbones, almond-shaped eyes, spiky lashes, and full lips that I dreamed of too many times in my teen years. Her body had changed too. She was taller by an inch or two, the top of her head coming to my shoulders, and there were new curves that I didn't remember from the summer after her high school graduation. But four years was a long time, and I was sure I was different too. One thing hadn't changed, though—our explosive reaction to each other. Mistrust lingered between us, and we would have to work through it to make the best of the situation.

I needed to clean the bathroom, and her blood had saturated my shirt and caused it to adhere to my skin, so I went to the main room and lay a clean towel over the white duvet. Then I gently lifted her out of the tub.

Her eyes went wide, and she reared forward. "What are you doing?" Distrust pulled her features taut.

I forced myself to answer calmly, but her immediate sense of flight or flight was clear—and insulting. There was no reason for her not to trust me, but I did make note of it. I couldn't assume she wouldn't try to run away when I left the room. "I'm moving you to the bed."

After I transferred her bandaged and mostly clean body to the bed, her mistrustful gaze tracked my every move. I stood over her for a moment, watching the agitated rise and fall of her chest. There was something in her expression that I couldn't name, a mix of worry and determination that I hadn't witnessed in her before.

When she spoke, I understood. "Are you here to kill me too?"

CHAPTER FOUR

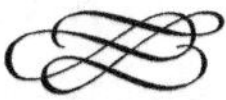

ELENA

"If I were here to kill you, then you would already be dead." Marco's deep voice sent a volley of goose bumps dancing over my arms.

So why was I here? My head swam with confusion, and the blood loss made me weak. There was an unnatural heaviness to my limbs, and all I wanted to do was sleep, but that wasn't smart. We didn't trust each other. I had to stay sharp and escape when there was an opportunity, most likely when he wasn't in the room.

Not only was I at a physical disadvantage from my injury, but my body was agitated despite its refusal to respond. Marco and I had a weird relationship regardless of my friendship with his sister, Sofia. When it came to Marco, my body was a traitor. He'd never given me any indication that there would ever be anything other distrust between us, and he'd always managed to push my buttons when we were kids.

He was aloof, removed. Not necessarily when he was with his siblings, but with anyone else. Raised to take over an empire, he had the instincts of a killer, and he moved like one too—silent, melding into the shadows, and striking with deadly force and little to no noise when possible. Out of the four La Rosa siblings, Marco and Nico were the most reserved. The two youngest, Trey and Sofia, were not.

Warmth from Marco's rough hand on mine distracted me from my sluggish thoughts. He was so close, and it was affecting me in ways I didn't want to admit to him or to myself. He extended my arm with care before something cold encircled my wrist, and I sucked in a breath, his intoxicating smell infiltrating my weak barriers, further confusing my loopy brain. "What the hell are you doing?"

He had secured my wrist to the bedpost with handcuffs.

He stood, and I bared my teeth. "Why are you doing this?"

His gaze crawled over me, and tingles erupted as he brushed some of my hair back from my cheek, tucking it behind my ear. "Because I don't trust you to stay here while I take a shower."

I tensed as he backed away then pivoted to head into the bathroom. There was a rustle of clothing as it dropped to the floor then the sound of the shower turning on. He'd left the door ajar, but I couldn't see into the room. *What is going on? Nothing makes sense.* His touch conflicted with his words. I didn't know how to process his gentleness combined with mistrust as tangible as the handcuff encircling my wrist.

My phone vibrated in my bag, distracting me from Marco's confusing actions. He'd left my backpack open and on the bed, only removing the first aid kit and my gun. *But not my phone. That, I can reach.*

Stretching my free arm and ignoring the twinge in my leg, I was able to pinch the corner of my bag and inch it closer. As soon as I had enough of a grasp on it, I slipped my hand inside and rooted around until my fingers closed around my phone. Pulling it out, I glanced at the screen. It was Sofia again. She'd been trying to reach me since early morning. Now, I knew why.

I tapped her contact and pressed the phone to my ear. "Why

is Marco here?" I asked in a harsh whisper. No need to let him know what I was doing.

"Wow, that's the greeting I get after how many years?"

Sofia's animated voice brought a smile to my face. I missed her. Out of all my friends from Chicago, she'd always been my favorite. "Hi, Sof. Missed you too."

She huffed before launching in to why she had been frantically calling. "I wanted to warn you that Marco was on his way, but he's with you, huh?" She didn't wait for me to answer. "You guys always had a weird relationship, and I'm not sure he's thinking straight. I reminded him you were our friend, but I—"

"Was worried. Yeah, I should have called you sooner. He found me."

"Are you okay? Is he being an ass?"

"Yes to both."

"Put him on the phone," she demanded.

"He's in the shower and has me handcuffed to the bed so I won't escape."

"Uh, I'm not sure what that's supposed to mean."

"Not anything good." I mentally rolled my eyes at her.

"Okay, then."

Her awkwardness about the handcuffs was obvious, and I chuckled.

"When he's out, I want to talk to him." Her words were sharp, and I looked forward to watching his expression when she laid into him. "But since we have time, I need to catch you up on a few things."

Alarm shot through my body at her tone. It wasn't typical bubbly Sofia that I'd known in the past, but a timid version— something I didn't think was in her character. "What happened?" *Does it have to do with why Marco is here instead of her?*

"I married Enzo. Please don't hate me, El. I know you were supposed to marry him."

Laughter bubbled up from my throat. Marrying Enzo was

the absolute last thing on my mind. "Sofia, as long as you're happy, I'm happy. It was an arranged marriage, one I never agreed to. And while Enzo is a great guy, he and I never had the connection that the two of you did. Trust me, I couldn't care less about that marriage contract."

"Yeah, well, you might."

That didn't sound good. "Why? What did Antonio do?"

"Nothing. He's dead. It was Max."

"What? Who's Max? And is Mama okay? What the hell is going on, Sof?" Antonio's death didn't upset me, so I didn't ask about him. He was Nicole's husband, the boss of the Caruso family, and more of a guardian—a hands-off one, thankfully. He was scary, and I'd always been wary around him. I didn't think of him as Dad and had never called him that. He wouldn't have wanted me to. Besides, he had Tony. And in a way, Nicole had me. Her relationship with her son, Tony, was... difficult, strained.

I'd never heard of Max and didn't really care who he was. I would deal with that later. It was the Russians I needed to know about—well, that and whatever Marco's intentions were with my life.

"Nicole is doing amazing. God, there is so much you need to know. Max is Antonio's eldest. He was living in Italy most of his life. He sent Marco because you're not safe. Ivan—"

"Katya texted me to go home." It seemed Ivan was a real problem. That had to be why Katya had found me. "He's here, isn't he?" It was well known that Ivan, the first-born son of Bratva boss Yuri Pavlov, was a monster. Because of that, I was glad Marco was with me, and I wouldn't have to run from Ivan without help.

"No. Ivan is dead. Before he died, he was looking for you. I don't know who's been sent in his place, but someone has. You're the target."

I knew that I was the one the Russians were after. It was why

Nicole swooped in and tried to protect me with her family when my mother was killed. Because the Bratva didn't just murder their target, they killed the family and any of their loved ones' enemies. "You know that's why I left. Because they were coming for me."

There was a beat of silence. "That's not what Katya originally said."

I blinked back tears because I remembered what she'd told Sofia, and it wasn't the truth. The human traffickers who had taken Emiliana, our friend and fellow Mafia princess, weren't after me. Katya wouldn't have come if that was it. No, she'd had information about the Bratva's pending attack, and even though I couldn't understand why, she was watching out for me and hid the real reason behind Emiliana's disappearance.

Why Katya had helped me was still a mystery. I didn't know what her angle was or what type of payment would eventually be called due, but I had no doubt it would be some request that I might not want to honor, especially if it was because she needed an in with the Italians. I didn't want any of my friends to die because of me.

Marco was right not to trust me. I wasn't even sure how I could keep them safe if Katya came to me with an ultimatum for the four years I'd escaped death because of her help.

"It doesn't matter, not now. Marco was sent to bring you back," Sofia said after a long pause.

My attention snapped back from the past just as the water from the shower shut off. "Why?"

Movement caught my eye, and my focus jolted to the doorway where Marco stood with only a towel wrapped around his narrow hips. My mouth went dry, and all I heard in my ear was something like wah-wah-wah as Sofia spoke, none of the words registering because of the sight before me. He'd gotten new tats across his chest and covering his arm, forming an intricate sleeve of dark artwork. He was... breathtaking.

It'd been a long time since I'd seen him without a shirt on, and he'd changed, filled out even more. I'd noticed when he'd arrived in my room, but this was a whole other level, and I couldn't tear my eyes from him. I bypassed his dark hair and intense green eyes to travel along his wide, defined shoulders then to his eight-pack of chiseled abdominal muscles. *What would it be like to run my fingers over those?*

A deep rumble sounded, and my gaze jumped back to his narrowed eyes. In long strides, he was at the side of the bed. When his arm shot out, I flinched and tried to move away, but his fingers curled around my phone, prying it from my grasp. He pressed it against his ear and barked, "Who is this?"

I could hear Sofia yelling from where I was stuck on the bed, and a grin stretched my mouth wide. I knew she would give him hell. I'd witnessed it on several occasions at her house when I was younger. She and her brothers usually got along great, but a few things would ignite her, and when that happened, I saw actual fear in their eyes. Which was kind of funny, considering that they were always much bigger than her barely five-foot-four firecracker of a body.

Marco's eyes held mine, and I shivered at his intensity. "Stay out of this, Sofia." Then he disconnected the call.

What just happened? I had expected a reaction, a loosening of his resolve from her tongue-lashing. "You're aware there will be hell to pay from her." I must have been going into shock—not from my wound, which I'd all but forgotten about, but because of how different Marco was, how much he'd changed.

"My sister is the least of your concerns." He grabbed my bag, stuffed my phone back into it, then dropped it onto a chair too far away for me to reach. "After I get dressed, we're leaving."

I leaned back until my head was on the pillow, exhausted from the adrenaline rush of being chased and shot. "Why can't we stay here?"

"You know why." There was a knock at the door. Marco

grabbed his gun before he went to open it. He murmured something before shutting and locking it again.

In his hand, he held a black long-sleeved shirt and a pair of black pants that looked like they would fit me. *When had he called for clothes?*

"I texted Sofia to have clothes sent here. She did it before calling you."

"Are you going to unlock this so I can change?"

A smirk played at the corners of his mouth, and I narrowed my eyes.

"Or I could help you."

What the hell is going on? "Ah, no. Thanks, but I can manage."

He disappeared in the bathroom for a minute, emerging with his jeans on and nothing else. His shirt had to have been soaked with my blood. My pulse was working overtime. I didn't think I could handle much more of this. I was too attracted to him, and it was so not a good idea to get involved. Besides, he hated me.

His shirt had blood on it from my leg, and my jeans were the same and destroyed from him cutting them just above the gunshot wound. It was a good thing he'd gotten new clothes sent over, but I didn't understand why we couldn't just sleep for a few hours. And order room service. I had zero energy. I could have gone for some orange juice.

When he rounded the bed to where I was, pulling a tight black shirt over his head, I stiffened.

"I'll change in the bathroom if you'll uncuff me."

Then his hands were on my wrist, holding it as he unlocked then slid the metal off. I went to stand, but the hand on my shoulder kept me in place.

"I'm going to help you. You lost a lot of blood, and if you get up and try to do this by yourself, you'll end up falling and risking reinjury."

He wasn't wrong, although the idea of him helping made me

feel vulnerable, and I didn't like it. When he moved toward the button on my jeans, I knocked his hand away. "I've got it." My fingers shook as I undid the zipper then stopped, unsure how I would slide the material down my hips without using my leg, which was currently throbbing. Sweat beaded along my hairline, and I hoped he didn't notice.

Then his warm, large hands were curling around my waist, and he lifted me to my feet as if I weighed nothing. Black dots crowded my vision, and I clamped my lips together, too afraid that I would do or say something embarrassing if I opened my mouth. He tapped my uninjured thigh.

"Keep your weight on this leg."

Seemed like a no-brainer. My hands went to his shoulders as he bent in front of me and carefully slid my jeans down so that they brushed against my bandaged leg with as little friction as possible. I distracted myself while he switched out my ruined jeans with the pants Sofia had sent up for me. Beneath my fingers, his shoulder muscles rolled and bunched as he moved. I wanted to run my hands over them, exploring, then bury my fingers in his short black hair. *Would it feel as silky as it looked?*

He maneuvered me back to the bed, and I sat on the edge before tying my shoes. He threw my backpack over one of his massive shoulders, tucked his gun in the waistband of his jeans, then helped me to stand with one arm around my waist, taking most of my weight.

The dots intensified, and I worried I would pass out. I didn't. It was so much worse. My body jolted, and my muscles locked then convulsed. Part of me was aware of Marco pulling me entirely onto the bed. As quick as the seizure-like convulsions started, they stopped.

"What's your name?" He barked out the question.

My frightened gaze met his. "Elena Caruso."

He pushed out a breath. "It's not a typical seizure. If it was, you wouldn't have been able to respond as quickly."

"What the hell was that, then?" Horror filled me. *Is something seriously wrong with me?*

"It's a nonepileptic seizure caused by a sudden change of blood supply to your brain. You'll be fine." He took water out of the mini fridge. "Drink this."

I took slow sips of the water with his help. Once I had downed the entire thing, he grabbed a candy bar, insisting that I have a few bites. My stomach was a mess of nerves, but I managed to choke down two mouthfuls. "How do you know what that was?"

"Trey recounted a similar situation one day after he got off work from the hospital. Someone who'd lost too much blood had the same thing happen. It stuck with me."

I sighed slowly. It was a good thing he was with me, or I would have been beyond frightened by what had just happened.

"How are you feeling?" His voice had gentled, and the concern that layered his words only heightened my embarrassment.

"Fine. Let's go." I wanted his intense focus off of me.

He stood, offering a hand to help me up, but my instincts kicked in. It wouldn't have been wise for me to leave looking like I did, in case the assassin from the alley had given a description of me before he approached. Marco had said there was a number he'd called or gotten a call from. I couldn't remember at the moment.

"Wait." I took my bag from him and pulled out the dishwater-blond wig. Part of me knew Marco was my best bet for survival, and if the Russian had called in my location and appearance, there was one thing I could do to change that.

I withdrew my makeup kit out and got to work, changing the color of my lips to a nude, so they blended rather than standing out while Marco gathered the bloody towels from the bathroom. I shoved my shorn hair into a neutral skullcap before I slipped on the wig. I left the brown contacts in but secured the blond hair to fall just below my shoulders in messy curls then made slight changes with shading to give my face an older appearance. I scrutinized everything in the handheld compact mirror before returning it all to my bag. I met Marco's surprised gaze before he grunted his approval then hid his reaction behind the stoic one he usually wore.

"We need to get to Manhattan, where my hotel is, and grab the rest of my gear before boarding the jet."

I knew the answer, but I wanted to hear him say it. "Why are we getting on the jet?"

"It's time for you to come home."

"Did Nicole send you?" I wasn't ready to talk about whoever Max was yet, but I missed Nicole. I would go to see her. "Is that where you're taking me?"

He ignored me until we were out of the room. As we passed by a maid's unattended cart, the vacuum humming in the room she was cleaning, he dumped the towels deep into the dirty linens section, covering them with a clean one he grabbed from the cart. When he was done, he wrapped his arm around my waist and led me down the hall. Neither of us said anything until we were alone in the elevator.

He looked me in the eye. "You'll be staying with me."

CHAPTER FIVE

MARCO

The trek from Hoboken to where I was staying in Manhattan was uneventful, just as we'd hoped. Along the way, Elena grabbed a ginger ale from a convenience store and insisted the clerk put it in a brown paper bag. It was smart. She drank from the bag, which gave the appearance of alcohol and was another layer to her disguise. Her fake drunken state also allowed me to keep my arm around her to help her walk.

Once in my hotel room, we didn't linger. I grabbed our bags and threw them over my shoulder. My arm snaked around her waist, and I glued her to my side, taking her weight so she wouldn't use her leg too much. We hailed a cab and headed to the airport, where the jet waited. From there, we boarded and pulled out of the gate almost immediately.

I left Elena rummaging through her backpack in one of the leather seats, though I'd taken her weapons. Those were securely stowed in my bag and stored in the bedroom at the end of the private jet. I gave the flight attendant instructions about food and drinks. By the time I reached Elena's side again, she had removed her makeup and left a stack of cleansing cloths piled on the table, saturated with the telltale signs of what had been on her face. Her wig and hair cap were off, and her black hair fell in a messy bedhead manner that framed her face.

I sat opposite her, my seat belt secure, as we taxied down the runway. Minutes passed until we were airborne then leveled off. Once we gained altitude, I got out of my seat, bent down, and swooped her into my arms, carrying her to the bed at the back of the plane. She didn't protest, which said a lot about how she was feeling.

As I lay her down on the tan comforter, the flight attendant entered the open doorway with a tray of food and drinks. I took it from her, thanked her, then shut the door. The only light in the small space was from the windows, which had the visors pulled down halfway. It was enough to see but dimly lit, private, and cozy.

I set the meal on the table next to her side then handed her half a sandwich. "You need to eat something."

She took it from me then put it down, picking up the orange juice instead and downing the entire glass without coming up for air. When she reclined against the pillow and met my gaze, defiance sparked in her red-rimmed oceanic eyes. She'd removed her contacts, and I was momentarily speechless. I hadn't forgotten the effect her eyes had on me, but they'd taken me by surprise.

"I needed the juice more than anything." She shrugged, her eyelids drooping. "I'll eat later."

Her words snapped me out of my stupor, and I frowned but backed down, vowing to press the issue in an hour or so. It was obvious she required sleep, but there were things to discuss. "We have to talk about what you'll be walking into when we're back in Chicago."

She smothered a yawn as I joined her on the bed, since there weren't any chairs in that part of the plane. She was exhausted and needed rest and recovery, but we had about two hours before we landed and a hell of a lot to discuss.

"Why are you so angry with me?" Her voice was soft, exhaustion weighing down the words. "I don't mean our normal animosity toward each other. There's something new, and I can't figure out where it's coming from."

There was no more holding back. She would find out eventually. It was better I told her now. "My sister was tortured because of you."

"What?" Her head snapped back, hitting the headboard.

"Ivan got her away from us. He tortured her for hours with the sole purpose of learning where you were." I leaned closer, locking my furious gaze with her shocked one. "She never broke, no matter what he did."

"I—"

"Imagine my surprise—all of ours—that you were alive and Sofia had helped you hide."

Tears filled her eyes, a few drops spilling over her lower lids. Her bottom lip trembled, and I hardened my heart against her pain. "I had no idea. If I'd known she was in danger, I would have come out of hiding."

I snorted. I didn't believe it for one second. "I know you've wondered why I was the one to come and why Sofia didn't come to get you or warn you about the Russians knowing you were alive."

She flinched then lifted her chin, her anger clearly rekindled, the gold flecks around her pupils turning molten with her watery eyes.

"We wouldn't have let Sofia leave the protection of the families. You've put my sister in danger, and the last thing we wanted was for her to be a bigger target to the Bratva."

"If I had known, I would have made a point of being sighted so they would leave her out of it. When I left, we were sure there was no trail connecting us. I never would have intentionally put her in harm's way."

I was angry about what had happened to Sofia, for sure, but also because Elena had felt she had to run away rather than reach out for help. She had connections. There was no reason for her to have run. I would have done everything within my power to keep her safe, but I knew she wasn't aware of the depth of my feelings for her. I'd hidden it behind teasing and tormenting her when we were growing up. I'd wanted what I knew I couldn't have, and that was how I'd dealt with it, right or wrong.

"You know I wouldn't have done anything to hurt her. Despite the crappy relationship you and I had, mine and Sofia's was solid."

"None of that matters. I agreed to bring you home and to take charge of your protection."

"Why? Wouldn't Nicole or Tony have a say?"

"Not anymore. Max is back and heads the Caruso family."

"Sofia mentioned him, but I've never heard his name before. Who the hell is Max?" Her voice rose to nearly hysterical levels.

I was aware I was dumping things on her without explanation and she was overwhelmed. A twinge of regret and worry worked its way into my mind. She only needed vital points, and I wasn't in the mood to go over everything that'd changed over the past handful of years. "Max was Antonio's eldest son. He's boss and wants you home. Safe. When he approached me, I..." *Volunteered.* I wasn't ready to admit that to her yet.

"But you hate me." Her features were contorted in surprise.

It made sense—objectively, there was no clear reason for me to help her. We'd had a volatile relationship when we were younger, but I hadn't thought she perceived me so negatively. I chose to ignore her comment. "How much do you know about what's happened since you left?"

She pushed out a breath, waited a beat, then must have

decided to drop the subject of why I was helping. "Only what Sofia told me when she called while we were at the hotel. That's the first time I've spoken to anyone from my old life in four years. She told me Antonio was dead and that she and Enzo were married. Nothing about Max except he's Antonio's eldest and is back from Italy."

"How do you feel about Enzo and Sofia? I know you were supposed to marry him someday."

She shrugged. "I don't feel anything. Maybe relief. I don't know if I could have gone through with it."

She'd been gone too long. "It was a Mafia contract. You wouldn't have had a choice." She should have known that and been able to imagine the dire consequences.

The scowl that crossed her features told me what she thought about those rules. "Enzo and Sofia had always been into each other. It wouldn't have been right. And I thought of him more like a friend than anything else. Why? Are you mad about Sofia and Enz?"

I slowly shook my head. My sister being married was strange, but I wasn't going to share the real reason I was okay with it. "There's no fighting what those two have. My sister is happy. That's all that matters."

"I guess Max sent for me, then? Why does he care what happens to me? We don't know each other, and I'm not his real sister."

"He doesn't work that way. Nicole says you're her daughter, and he's treating you as if you're his sister. End of story."

"But he put you in charge of me." Her lips tightened. "If he had strong feelings about me, wouldn't he have come himself?"

"He married Lil. With what happened to Sofia, there's no way Max would risk leaving Lil."

"Is Lil happy? Is that what she wanted?" She pushed up on an elbow, her eyes wide.

"Yeah. They're good together. A lot has happened since you've been gone. Most of it good. Some, not so much."

She blew out a breath. "Yeah, I get it. That's Mafia life."

We hit some turbulence before the plane resumed its smooth course. I tilted my head, observing her closely. "It's not a bad life, El. We fight hard but love harder. Family is everything. Have you been out so long that you don't remember that part?"

"No, I remember. It's just that living on my own, things were simpler."

"It doesn't alter the blood running through your veins. You're one of us. That'll never change."

She lowered her head onto her bent arm. A slight grimace flashed across her face when she shifted. I put my pillow next to her body, carefully moving her injured leg so that it was off her other one and resting on the pillow instead. There was no reason for her to be so uncomfortable. I went to where we kept the first aid on the plane and withdrew what I needed. I couldn't keep dumping things on her. She needed some time to process and rest so she could start to heal. "I'm going to give you a shot to dull the pain. It'll knock you out."

"What? No. I don't want to be unconscious."

I rubbed my forehead, regretting how harshly I'd treated her. "I promise that I'll watch over you, keep you safe. If you don't believe me, we can swear a blood oath."

Her teeth worried her bottom lip, and she gazed at me warily. "No. I don't need it. Go ahead and give it to me. Besides" —a mischievous glint lightened her eyes—"Sofia knows you're with me, and there will be hell to pay if you try to hurt me."

I chuckled. That wasn't entirely true. My sister had a lot of pull, but we were all older now, and she'd been gone for years. I prepped the shot, swabbed her skin, then administered the sedative. "Get some rest. We can talk more when we're home."

After a few minutes, her eyelids drifted shut, and I barely heard her mumbled words as she fell asleep. She'd said she didn't have a home, and my heart ached for her. I could see why she would have thought that, but she was mistaken. Max might have been the head of her family, but that was not where she belonged anymore. I clasped her hand in mine then reclined next to her on the bed, content for the first time since she'd been taken from me. She was wrong about not belonging, but she did. Her place was with me.

CHAPTER SIX

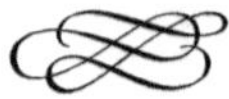

ELENA

can't move. I awoke in a strange bed, facing a wall of windows. The accordion glass doors were open to bring outside living in, showcasing miles of rolling waves. Comforting heat warmed my back, and I scrunched my eyebrows, trying to piece together what had happened. My thoughts were slow, crawling through the fog in my brain that could only have come from drugs of some sort. Oh, right. Marco had given me a shot, something to help me sleep and block the pain from the gunshot wound in my leg.

When I inhaled, warm spice filled my senses, telling me who was behind me and holding me close. I kept my breathing regulated, trying not to disturb or alert him to the fact that I was awake. I could tell it was early in the morning from the sun peeking over the horizon.

I must have been really out of it if he transported me from the jet to his place without me waking even once. The fogginess of my thoughts and the cottony taste in my mouth meant he'd given me a strong sedative. I wanted to be mad at him for it, but he had clearly waited for me to consent, and I'd agreed. Besides, I'd gotten the rest I'd needed.

The rise and fall of Marco's chest at my back remained even. His arm wrapped around my waist, and it was oddly comforting despite the pads of his fingers resting beneath my shirt and on the scar from where I was shot as a kid. His touch there brought back an avalanche of memories, and I found myself hurdled back to being six years old. On that particular day, Nicole had taken me to the park to play with the other Mafia kids from the Five Families.

I'd been with Nicole, who'd insisted I call her Mama, and Antonio for almost a year already. My birth mother was gone, murdered, and after a while, calling Nicole a slight variation to that name felt natural. Besides, she loved me and made sure to show me in so many little ways, from playing dolls to having tea parties and baking cookies, just to name a few. As often as she could, she arranged for me to play with the other girls close to my age, Sofia, Lil, Marissa, Emiliana, and Eva.

Adopted into their family, I'd gained a brother, but Tony didn't want anything to do with me. He made my new mama sad. I could see it in her eyes when he rejected her more often than not, preferring to be around Antonio. Both Antonio and Tony made me nervous. I preferred to stay by her side instead, and I knew it made her happy.

Nothing about the day she took me to the playground was unusual until later. I sank deeper into the memory, suddenly seeing things through the eyes of my six-year-old self, experiencing the buzzing excitement of playing at the park with my friends.

Mama had taken me there before Sofia arrived, but it was fine. The grass was soft, and it tickled my feet as I ran over to where Marissa and Camila were swinging. Tony had come with us but ditched me at the first chance. I was okay with that because he was often mean to me. He and Alfonso, Marissa and Camila's brother, didn't like girls, which seemed weird in a lot of ways. Alfonso's older brother, Stefano, was nice to us, but he wasn't there that day.

I glanced at the boys. Alfonso was playing with a stick, probably torturing a bug. He and my brother did things like that.

Enzo said hi, and I skidded to a stop far enough away from Marissa's legs as she pumped them to go higher. I wrapped my hands around the swing set pole then said hi back. "Where's Em?" I liked to play with Emiliana, his sister. She cooked with her mom a lot, and sometimes, they would come over, and we would bake cookies together, our moms supervising nearby.

He shrugged. "She's sick."

"Oh." I pushed away from the pole and settled on one of the swings.

We both turned as a car pulled up, and more guards spilled out. Then Sofia and her mom stepped from the car, and I waited to see who else came out, but no one did. Her brothers hadn't come, and I was a little sad about that. They were fun, and her oldest brother, Marco, kept Tony and Alfonso away from Sofia and me. So did Enzo, but I liked it better when Marco was there.

I skipped over to meet Sofia as she ran to us. I slipped my hand into hers when she said hi.

"I like your dress!" Marissa shouted to Sofia.

It was pretty with its ballerina skirt and tiny flowers. I wore shorts and a flowered pink tee. We matched. I glanced once more over by the moms to make sure Nicole was there. It didn't matter how much I liked my friends. I was always afraid she would disappear, that something horrible would happen to her like it had to my birth mother. Sof squeezed my hand, and I grinned at her. Even though I felt different and a little out of place, she made me feel better.

When Sofia asked Enzo the same question about his sister that I had, I dropped my hand and went over to the swings. I'd seen that look on her face before. She wanted to play with Enzo and not the rest of us. I didn't want to be a baby, so I hung out with Marissa, since Lil and Emiliana weren't there. Camila was a little older, and I hadn't been around her as much as the others.

There was a scream, and I jerked toward the sound, unsure if I should run or not. My gaze darted everywhere until it landed on Camila. She'd fallen and burst into tears. I held still, digging my toes into the woodchips, unmoving on the swing, as her mom came over. She pulled Camila into her arms then called for Alfonso and Marissa. I moved to the side near Sofia, unsure what to do. My eyes watered, and I wanted to cry, too, because Camila was bleeding. She'd scraped her knees badly.

I slipped my hand into Sofia's and leaned into her as Camila's mom snapped at Alfonso to join them. Enzo came running with him, but Tony stayed near the slides. He never listened. I didn't like him or Alfonso, but they were sort of family, just with a different last name and different parents. At least that was what Mama said—we were the Five Families, and that linked us together.

When Sofia's fingers tightened, mine did too. I shivered. My stomach churned because I felt it. Something was wrong—not with Camila but with the men who watched over us. There was a different feeling in the air, and I knew we weren't safe anymore, no matter how many guards our moms had brought. Then there were loud popping sounds, and one of them fell over by the bushes on the edge of the park.

It was a sound I'd heard every night in my dreams since my birth mom had died.

I frantically searched for Nicole. *Please be okay.* I froze, not moving when Sofia pulled her hand from mine. The moms were shouting, screaming for us to come to them. Everyone was running, and gunfire rained down on us. The guards nearby had guns in their hands, but some were on the ground, unmoving, and I knew they were hurt or dead. The others fired back. I couldn't move.

The sound of the guns brought back my birth mother's screams. She'd known the Russians were coming for her and had hidden me in a kitchen cabinet. We'd run the time before, but she said there wasn't time and that no matter what happened, I wasn't to make a sound.

It was happening again. My throat tightened. My body trembled, and I thought I would be sick. I covered my mouth with my hand, and my eyes locked on Nicole, my new mama.

I couldn't move. Things were going too fast but also too slow. Alfonso was there. His mom clutched Marissa and Camila as she tried to grab him.

He was just out of reach from her but not from me. His back was to me, partially blocking my view of my mama. He was so close that I could touch him. I raised my hand as his mom's eyes went wide and all the color drained from her face. Her lip trembled, and so did mine. I knew what was coming from the horror on her face.

I cringed at the shouts and screams, the gunshots all around us. Scary men in black with guns were everywhere. Tears streamed down my face. Then Alfonso stumbled toward me. He jerked again and again. Red colored his shirt, splashing his neck. Something hit my side, and when I glanced down, there was red on my pink shirt too. My hand shook as I touched the wetness, confused about why it was there. Someone screamed. Alfonso fell against me. Sofia's hand tugged mine, but I couldn't move. Then I lost track of her and Enzo. They were near me one minute then gone the next.

Alfonso's body was heavy as he fell into me, pushing mine toward the ground more quickly. My head hit the swing set pole, and black spots danced around the edges of my sight. Alfonso lay over me, and my side hurt badly. That was the last thing I remembered from that day.

I drew in a steadying breath as the horror of what happened when I was six left the forefront of my mind. We'd lost Alfonso. I had survived. They'd thought I wouldn't make it—a bullet had pierced my side. I'd lain in a pool of Alfonso's blood with his body half on me. At the park, they'd thought I was dead too.

The attack had been meant for me. The Russians wanted me dead after they'd learned of my existence after killing my mother and finding my toys at our place.

After that terrible experience, Mama had dyed my hair from brown with caramel highlights to black to help keep me safe. It was something we did together over the years, and I'd thought it was a cool mother-daughter-bonding thing. And it was, but the main reason we did it was disguise. I'd stopped going to parks, and as my friends and I grew up, I stayed close to Mama's side, only playing with Sofia, Em, Lil, and Marissa inside their houses, rarely outside.

I let go of that terrible day, blinking the room into focus. I had to have been in Marco's home—that was the only explanation that made sense. The sky was a tad lighter. Given the view outside the glass doors, it was clear we were somewhere on the waterfront. He'd said we were going home, which meant Chicago, so that was Lake Michigan. *Since when does he have a place on the lake?*

With great care and slowness, I turned in his arms until I was on my back, my head angled to face his. Unguarded, I studied his breathtaking features. Lashes that were too long and thick to belong to a man fanned across his high cheekbones. He had the stunning good looks that everyone in his family shared, but he took after his mom with his black hair and vivid green eyes, whereas his siblings did not. His jaw was angular and sharp enough to cut glass. Even given how pretty his lashes and eyes were, he was masculine to the core. And my core tightened, reminding me how very attracted I was to him.

My leg ached, and I wanted to move to find a better position but held myself in place. I wasn't ready to wake Marco. The sleeping version of him showed me a rare moment of vulnerability that I wasn't sure I would see again. I was pretty comfortable other than my leg, but I wondered why my legs were bare against the Egyptian cotton sheets. I pinched the sheet with my index finger and thumb and lifted it just enough to get a peek beneath the covers and to the side. Tiny blue sleep shorts met my vision. *Had he undressed me?* My cheeks heated, and I jerked my gaze back to his face, dropping the sheet back into place. At least he'd left me in the same black T-shirt from the day before. *Little things... I guess.*

I worried my lower lip. *How am I going to get out of this bed?* My leg was injured, and I knew it would be sore to walk on, making me slow as molasses. And if I even managed to drag his behemoth arm from my waist, the awkwardness of how I would move would surely wake him. I wouldn't get far, if even off the bed with its luxurious sheets and pillowy softness. *Do I even want to move?*

My instincts flared, and I glanced at him again, unsure if he was still asleep. He was so prickly when awake. It made the possessive way he held me confusing. It hadn't always been that way. I remembered plenty of times when he'd stood up for me against Tony when he blamed me for Alfonso's death. No one else had said a word. I knew it was the truth, that it was my fault, but I was terrified to voice it. Mama was fierce and wouldn't let anyone make me feel bad about his death. Marco had rivaled her in defending me. And if I fell and he was around, he always picked me up, made me laugh, then got me a Band-Aid if I needed one. It was during those years, when he was kind and protective, that I had developed a crush on him.

I'd felt safe when he was around.

Everything changed in middle school. He'd been doing more stuff for his dad and training to become boss someday. It hurt when he pulled away, and I would do anything to get his attention, even if it was negative, and our interactions evolved from there. Not a lot had changed since before I left. We still pushed each other's buttons.

I did another sweep of the room, taking in what I could from my position on the bed. The walls were a cool blueish gray, the sheets a buttery cream, and the bedspread a dark gray. A comfortable-looking off-white chair with an ottoman took up one corner near the door to the balcony. A narrow piece of furniture sat directly opposite the end of the bed. My guess was that a flat-screen TV rose from the top at the touch of a button. It seemed like something Marco would have, especially since I knew he had one in high school, which I found on one of my excursions into his room to snoop when he wasn't home.

When I turned back, my heart skipped a beat. Bright-green eyes met mine, and a slight curve graced Marco's kissable lips.

"Morning." His voice was low and rough, and I barely contained the full-body shiver I felt from the sexiness of it.

"Morning." I, on the other hand, sounded like a frog. Lovely.

"Time to get up. We have somewhere to be this morning."

I could tell by the way his eyes danced with mirth that he wasn't going to share what or where we were expected, and I couldn't help but wonder what fresh hell was headed my way.

CHAPTER SEVEN

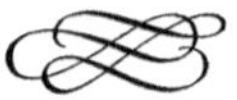

ELENA

Marco helped me up from bed and to the bathroom, and I did everything I could not to react to how his sinfully strong hands felt. It was so embarrassing. I couldn't even look at him. My face was on fire because I knew he'd been the one to put the sleep shorts on me, which looked suspiciously like something of Sofia's.

"Do you need help in here?" He lingered by the sink where I rested a hip, sucking up all the space in the large master bath.

"Nope. I'm good."

He grinned, and that mischievous glimmer flashed in his eyes, making me pay close attention to what he had up his sleeve. Then he motioned to a garment bag I hadn't noticed before. "That's for you. Sofia dropped it off when I called her from the jet. You have thirty minutes, and then we have to leave."

I frowned, suddenly annoyed by the lack of information and the expectations he was setting for me. "How am I supposed to get ready that fast? And where are we going?"

When he stepped closer, his hand falling to my hip, my body almost melted and met him halfway. But I held firm and didn't give in to my traitorous reactions, no matter how good he smelled.

"I know you can do it, Little Thief. If you can get in and out of a house with a top-notch security system, you can shower and dress with time to spare."

My head snapped back. *He knows what I did at night for Danny's security business.* "How long did you know I was there?"

"Only a few days or I would have come sooner." He brushed my hair behind my ear, his fingers grazing the skin on my neck and making me shiver. It was impossible not to when he was this close and touching me. *What is going on? One second, he's cold and exactly like he'd been for my entire high school existence, and now he's flirting with me?* "Clock is ticking."

I didn't move for a solid minute after he left the bathroom and shut the door behind him. Unable to resist, I hobbled over to the garment bag and unzipped it. What met my sight almost brought me to my knees. It was a wedding dress made of soft eggshell satin with spaghetti straps. I pulled it from the bag, still on the hanger. It was floor length with a skirt that would flair out if I spun. The satin material made it hang like a waterfall of silk, and I knew it would conform to me then move in cascading ripples. The dress was simple and elegant, but the design was so sensual that it was magnetic even on the hanger.

Who is Marco marrying me off to? It can't be him. Or can it?

Any weight on my leg was painful, but I managed to shower and do my hair. I rummaged around in the cabinets and found a first aid kit. It made sense. I had them in the bathroom and kitchen at home. Stashing them in multiple places was smart. I swapped out the two bandages that covered my wounds with dry ones. My skin was surgically glued, so it was all good, but I preferred the added protection.

Since my hair wasn't halfway down my back anymore, it didn't take me long to style it, and I took care of it with the hairdryer. After a few swipes of mascara and lipstick, I called my appearance good. My fingers were itching to get ahold of that dress, which Sofia no doubt made. I remembered how much she'd loved to design clothes—she always had some sewing project going on when we were growing up. And then there were the deadly pants, which concealed weapons while still maintaining style and comfort, that she'd given me the day she helped me go into hiding.

She was gifted, and I bet she'd done something with her talent. I hadn't followed anyone from my past in the news or on social media because it wasn't smart. But I wished I knew a little about what they'd been up to while I was away. I'd missed them.

I carefully put the dress on, zipped up the hidden side zipper, then stood before the mirror in shock. The way the dress conformed to me yet moved with fluidity was decadent and luxurious. I'd never looked so good. A crimson shawl made of satin hung on a separate hanger. It was light and airy but would help maintain some of my body heat when we were outside, going from the car to the building.

I only wished Mama was there and would be a part of my wedding… and that I knew who the groom was. The only thing I knew without a doubt was that I didn't have a choice in the matter. My previous marriage contract might have been nullified, but there was a new one in place. With the Russians on my back, I guessed that my family wanted to ensure I was safe with another level of protection in the form of a Mafia boss as my husband.

Butterflies took flight as I stepped out of the bathroom and made my way slowly through the bedroom, following the alluring scent of coffee. The hallway opened into a spacious living room, dining room, and kitchen combo with another incredible view of the lake. Marco had his back to me, and I took a moment to appreciate how his shirt stretched across his broad shoulders.

"There's coffee on the island for you."

I moved forward as if lured by a pied piper, but I wasn't sure whether the coffee or Marco drew me more strongly. I was going with the drink. That made more sense.

Then he turned. Chills danced along my exposed skin at the look of raw hunger that pulled his arresting features tight. The air was sucked out of the room, and my muscles tensed in anticipation of what he would do. His gaze moved from the top of my head, down to my feet, then back up again. Under the predatory gleam in his vivid-green eyes, I felt like prey.

"You look beautiful, El."

"Thank you." I felt myself blush again. *Why?* I never blushed. But two days with Marco, and I had a handful of times already. "Did Sofia make this?"

He nodded. "She brought it over before we got here. You'll see her soon but not at the church. It's too risky for any of the girls to go there."

"Oh." I couldn't hide my disappointment. "What about Nicole?"

"She would skin me alive if she couldn't be there for her only daughter." His lips twitched.

I could see my fiery mama getting her way. She was incredibly sharp and could extract secrets from just about anyone without them realizing what they'd divulged. She'd told me it was a survival tactic and that secrets were currency. She didn't miss much. As I sipped my coffee, Marco told me we had to leave. His hand settled on my back, and we made our way to the car. After we were inside and he pulled onto the street, I glanced out the window but didn't register much of what I saw, as I let my mind wander to the night before I left, the last evening Mama and I had spent together.

We'd raided Antonio's favorite wines. Mama and I each had a bottle and were recovering from a fit of giggles over the naked scene from *The Proposal,* where the main characters collided then landed on top of each other. Old rom-coms were our guilty pleasure, and once a week, we got drunk on Antonio's wine while watching one.

I'd worn a brave face, but Mama could see the sadness in my eyes and was trying her best to fix it, even though she didn't know why. I wouldn't tell her. Not yet, and not everything. I couldn't. It would have put her at risk, and even though she wasn't my birth mom, she'd done everything she could for me. If I had a nightmare, she crawled into bed with me and read stories until I fell asleep. She was my mother in every sense of the word, my best friend and protector.

It was the last time we did that together. Emiliana's abduction was the red flag that they were coming for me. I would be forced to leave or pay with my life.

The wait wasn't long. Sofia had found me while I was on my run earlier that day and told me it was time. I would never have been ready to leave my people, but there was little choice.

I swiped at a tear before Mama saw it. But there wasn't much she didn't see. As she poured another glass of wine and we watched Sandra Bullock dance around the fire singing about balls, we devolved into a fit of laughter. When that subsided, I whispered the only gift I could to her. "Don't believe everything you hear. I'm more resourceful than that."

She turned to me, horror darkening her eyes. She knew. Antonio and Frank were talking more and more. Nicole was wickedly smart—a survivor, as she taught me to be. She would have caught onto whatever scheme they were hatching with the Russians. I hugged her tightly, hating that I would have to let her go, then whispered, "We have parts to play. Make them believe yours. Hold what I'm telling you in your heart alone."

The car stopped, and Marco's hand rested on my arm, snapping me out of the memory. I sucked in a breath before meeting his gaze. I didn't know why I hadn't asked who the groom was, but my nerves were getting the best of me, even though I was well aware I wouldn't have a choice in the matter. Max, who was supposedly my brother through my adopted family, was boss. He had control over my life in ways I wouldn't be able to fight. "Marco"—I waited until he turned to me—"who am I marrying?"

His hand curved around the back of my neck, and he drew me into his side then brushed his lips over mine in a gentle caress. When he leaned back, desire flared in his eyes. "Me."

My pulse jackhammered against the base of my neck, and his thumb rubbed across it in a slow back and forth. As unexpected as his touch had been, it was gone just as quickly, and he opened the door and climbed out of the car. I stayed in my seat as he went around to my side, opened the door, and held out a hand to help me up. A part of me had known it would be him, and that same part, which I kept padlocked in a box, loved him deeply. But my feelings were not reciprocated.

I had to protect myself as much as possible. I came to a decision in the time it took us to walk from the car to the front door of the ornate cathedral. That portion of me that felt different and removed from the Five Families would have to soar to the surface once again and guard my heart. Because if there was one thing I was sure of, if I let my guard down around Marco, I didn't think I would ever recover from the heartache that would follow.

The satin flats he'd slipped on my feet before we left his lakefront home made no noise as we crossed the wood floor from the heavy door into the cathedral. A soft glow from hundreds of candles flickered intermittently around the front pews and parapet, and tears pricked my eyes. It was beautiful, a scene from times past.

The priest waited at the end of the aisle, and a dark-haired, imposing man with an air of danger stood off to the side. If I had to go out on a limb, I would have guessed him to be Max, my new brother and boss of the Caruso family.

Marco bent and whispered in my ear, "It has become a tradition for this generation of bosses to marry their brides in this fashion. Even though I couldn't give you a grand wedding like a Mafia princess deserves, I could at least follow suit with how Lil, Emiliana, and Sofia were married."

"It's beautiful." My gaze jumped to the front pew when I heard a gasp. The blond woman who had been sitting there turned, and our gazes met. Mama. I couldn't hold back the tears any longer, and they fell in a river down my cheeks. She was on her feet and halfway down the aisle before I could take my next step. Marco's grip was secure on my waist, and he guided me toward her at a much slower pace.

"My baby girl!" Her twin rivers of free-flowing tears mirrored mine.

I found myself enveloped in her thin arms as my body shook from the emotion of our reunion. "I'm so sorry," I murmured as I squeezed her just as tightly as she was me. "I couldn't stay. Not without them coming and risking something horrible happening to you."

"Hush." Her raspy voice was thick with emotion. "I was aware of what was happening that night. And in my heart, I knew you'd be back when it was time."

Marco cleared his throat, and after another minute, we leaned back, laughing at the mess we'd made of our mascara. Mama shooed Marco away and told him to stand by Max because we needed to fix our faces, and she would walk me down the aisle in a few minutes. I swear Marco growled, but all it did was make Mama giggle. She pulled me to the side then whipped out a to-go pack of makeup wipes. We took turns fixing each other's raccoon eyes.

After she closed her clutch and tucked it under her arm, she took my hands in hers. "This is the right move, Baby Girl. Marco is a good man."

I nodded. Despite our issues, I knew she was right. "And Max? What do you know about him?" I was skeptical. I had never heard of him before Marco and Sofia mentioned his name.

"There's a long story there, but he's making our family better. We'll spend an evening catching up real soon. But now"—her mouth stretched into an infectious grin—"you have a man waiting to marry you."

I plastered on a smile that I was sure didn't reach my eyes as I threaded my arm through hers, and we made our way slowly down the aisle to where Marco and Max waited. *If only this marriage was real and not a binding agreement between two Mafia families.*

The actual ceremony was a blur. I answered the questions robotically and vaguely noted the amusement flashing through Marco's eyes. Before I knew what had happened, what I'd committed to, he slipped a platinum wedding band and an eight-carat solitaire engagement ring on my finger, drew me close, and pressed his lips to mine. The trance I was in broke, and I was intensely aware of how addictive and sensual his mouth felt.

It was over in a matter of seconds, and his mouth left mine much too soon. With care, he released me so that Mama could hug me. Then Max came forward and pulled me into his arms.

"I know we don't know each other, but I'd like to change that."

He smiled, and I sucked in a breath. He was damn good-looking. I saw Marco scowl out of the corner of my eye, and then he drew me back to his side and away from Max. His hand rested possessively on my hip. *What the heck was that?*

"We all need to go," Marco said.

"Not before we take a few pictures." Mama's mouth pressed into that determined line she rarely wore, but when it did, she meant business.

Marco relented, and Max offered to take the pictures. Marco and I took a picture together. Then I had one with Mama and one by myself. Max forwarded the photos to both Mama and Marco, who promised to send them to my new phone, which he said would be at the house.

"We'll see you back at your place." Mama squeezed my hand, and then Max was leading her out a side door. The priest had disappeared soon after we'd kissed. Being in the Mafia, I knew the process. He had been compensated well for the ceremony performed at the crack of dawn, and the church received a sizable donation. The legal documents would have been approved by one of the judges on our payroll. No doubt the marriage license was already filed.

I left on Marco's arm at a moderate pace, tolerating the pain in my leg but in a daze. I didn't feel married. I stole glances at him from beneath my lashes. He looked every inch the Mafia boss in his black suit and tie. I knew he had at least one gun on him, and his gaze swept the area. He'd stationed guards at the church's entrance, and more were waiting for us by his car. Once I was safely inside, he shut the passenger door then went around to his side. We were on the road in a matter of seconds, and a long procession of guards that I hadn't noticed on our way to the church followed us.

I was nervous, and my fingers toyed with the satiny skirt of my dress. I wasn't ready to be alone with him. "Now what?"

"We go home, and everyone comes over to celebrate."

I took the first full breath of the day. I could wholeheartedly get on board with that.

CHAPTER EIGHT

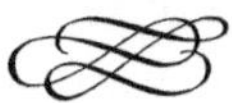

ELENA

We flew down the highway, bypassing the exit we should have taken to go to the lakefront place from the night before. I stretched out my legs in the roomy front seat, trying to ease the stiffness from the gunshot wound. My nerves pinged like mini firecrackers. I couldn't believe what had happened. *I married Marco.*

I couldn't make sense of how surreal everything was. On the one hand, it was a dream, as I'd crushed on him for as long as I could remember. But I never thought he reciprocated my feelings. There had been a few moments in the last few hours where he showed me kindness, even flirted. But then reality snapped back into place, and he probably realized he didn't like me. All that did was make me feel alone and as much of an outcast as I'd always been. An imposter, a pseudo Mafia princess. In truth, I was only a distant cousin, playing a role I wasn't born for in the way the others had been.

Marco relaxed in the driver's seat, and I took the time to study his profile. As usual, traitorous butterflies took flight when my gaze traveled over his defined jawline and chiseled features. But it was those eyes that drew me in the most. I could have drooled all night long over his muscular body, but the eyes —those were the windows to the soul, and I wanted to possess his more than anything else in Marco's body. If only things were different and his heart was truly mine, I would gladly accept my fate.

I recognized the route we were taking and wondered if we were headed to his parents' house. "Where are we going?"

"I have a house in the same subdivision as my parents. We're going there. The security is tight, and we'll have family showing up soon after we arrive."

"Will that be Sofia, Em, Lil, and Marissa?"

He took his gaze from the road and studied me for a moment. "Did you follow the news at all?"

"No. It was safer that I didn't ever look any of you up, especially on the internet. I couldn't risk someone finding me because I missed everyone. So no, as a rule, I did not."

"Marissa died right before winter break of her senior year in college."

"What?" My heart stopped, and tears sprang to my eyes as I gripped the edge of the seat. "What happened?"

"She was murdered. We suspected the Russians, but Frank never followed through to find out for sure and retaliate. He'd already married off one daughter to the enemy, and I think he wrote the other off as collateral damage."

"That's sick."

"It is. But Frank was a bastard that way." His eyes left the road to regard me once more before he faced forward once again. I hurriedly swiped the tears from my cheeks. "He's dead now too."

"Is Stefano boss?" My world was upside down, and I mourned the loss of Marissa. She'd been wild, free, and always so much fun. Her personality had been the perfect complement to my more controlled one. I would miss her forever.

"He is, and he recently married Emiliana."

"Christ. Everything's different. But she always had a thing for him."

"Even more after he rescued her from a human-trafficking ring."

Sofia had risked a single text to me a year ago, a simple "she's home." It had been enough for me to know Emiliana was back in the fold with family surrounding her, keeping her safe. Sofia had known how much I'd worried. We all had. Emiliana was one of us, and despite how removed I'd felt at times, the bond I had with her, Sof, Lil, and Marissa was ironclad. They would always accept me and had made that clear throughout our childhood.

"I can't get over how much has changed."

"You've been gone a little over four years, El." Marco's tone gentled. "But you're here now, and I promise you that I'll keep you safe so long as you never betray me."

I couldn't blame him for the jibe, but despite how much I tried to bite my tongue and keep quiet, the old me rose to the bait. "I'm not your puppet."

The corner of his mouth twitched.

I narrowed my gaze even more, ready to fight with him—I needed to after learning of all the changes and deaths.

"In the bedroom, you will be."

My head snapped back, and I bared my teeth. Something deep inside me shifted, heated, and I purred at the image he'd conjured. I slammed a lid on those thoughts and added a padlock to the box that held my secret desire for him. It had no place in the argument. "I bite."

Rich laughter filled the car, and he grinned at me. "I'm counting on it." Then he pulled into a long driveway, and I noticed the guards surrounding the huge mansion we were approaching.

How had I missed exiting the highway or even turning into the subdivision? It wasn't like me to forget to pay attention to my surroundings. I blamed Marco and his infuriating personality. I continued to stew in my fantasy plot of his downfall as he got out of the car then rounded to open my door. He extended his hand, and I reluctantly accepted his help in case my leg buckled after sitting in the car for half an hour.

He wrapped his arm around my waist and pulled me close as we walked up the few steps then entered the front door. I caught glimpses of the staff, who offered me shy smiles or simple nods. He must have told them he was bringing me home.

"I'll show you around, then you can change before our family gets here."

I let go of the petty anger he'd stirred in me and instead absorbed the grandeur of his home. "Who else lives here?" I expected him to say his brothers at the very least.

"No one. It's our home. I had it built last year. I knew it wasn't long until I took over as boss and would need my own residence. We have this place, the one in the city, and another in Italy."

My heart skipped several beats at "we." I couldn't believe I was married, let alone to Marco. *How is he accepting our situation so well?* I decided to confess what I was struggling with because a part of me remembered very well how close we had been before he'd turned into a jerk during his teen years. "I don't feel married. And I'm not sure how you're even remotely okay with being stuck with me. What did Max have on you to get you to agree?"

He chuckled then squeezed me a little tighter to his side. "He didn't have to twist my arm where you were concerned. I've always had feelings for you."

My head knocked back, and I met his gaze. "Of animosity."

"Well, there were reasons I pushed you away. Mainly because I'd learned you were promised to Enzo and couldn't be mine. It was easier to push your buttons, especially since you were so cute when mad."

"Yeah, cute. Sure, let's go with that. Remember when I snuck into your room and took things I knew would upset you?"

He chuckled. "You left them in the strangest places like the pantry. My favorite is still the pillows from my bed, floating in the pool. Then there was my Xbox on the roof. After I got over my anger, I was horrified that you'd been up there and could have fallen."

"It was how I coped, and letting you know that I could get to anything of yours without you doing a thing about it gave me a thrill I can't ever deny." I paused and forced him to look at me as we stood before floor-to-ceiling sliding doors that I knew would fold back to incorporate the incredible outdoor area seamlessly. I mean, there was a gourmet kitchen on one side, a beautiful pool, complete with a grotto, and a hot tub in the corner of the pool. It was paradise, and once it was open again and the weather was warmer, I could see myself losing hours—no, days poolside. "But you never indicated that you had feelings for me. So excuse me if I don't fully believe you."

"It's complicated." He smiled then opened the doors so we could go outside. I shivered in the chilly November air but wanted to see the backyard up close. Marco snuggled me into his side, and we toured the dream space before returning inside. The hot tub was still open, even though he'd had the pool winterized. As soon as my leg was healed and there was no risk of the surgical glue coming undone in hot water, I would head in with a bottle of wine.

We went through the dining room and the kitchen with its enormous marble island, oversized stainless steel fridge, and double ovens. Before I knew it, we headed for the back stairs, and he led me to a spacious master bedroom with a king-sized bed and a sitting area complete with a fireplace. The bathroom was a spa oasis, and I couldn't get over how gorgeous everything was. I fidgeted with the elegant folds of the skirt on my dress as my gaze darted back to the bed. We'd already "slept" together, but I didn't count that. I had been unconscious from whatever painkiller he'd given me. *How am I supposed to lie next to him at night?*

"Where am I going to sleep?"

He paused, his brows furrowed. "In here with me. You're my wife. Why would you be anywhere else?"

"Because we don't know each other anymore! It's been too long. We were just kids the last time I saw you. I'm not comfortable sharing a room or anything else with you."

When he closed the distance between us, I tensed but refused to step back. I had to tilt my head back to maintain eye contact. Then his hand was at my hip, the other sliding around my neck, burying his fingers in my hair. I couldn't have moved if I wanted to. Instead, I held my breath, waiting in anticipation for what he would do next.

His head dipped toward me in slow increments. Then his lips brushed over mine in a soft caress. His powerful body pressed against me, and I melted on contact. Only a small portion of my mind clung to any sort of sanity, but even that seemed drugged and sluggish.

His teeth scraped across my lower lip then gently tugged it before he soothed the same spot with another kiss, one I barely stopped from moaning. When he drew back, I had to catch myself from following those magical lips of his.

"I understand that we're strangers in a way." His deep voice rumbled over my hypersensitive skin. "I won't pressure you for more until we get to know one another again. But you will stay here with me. You're my wife and mine to protect."

I understood what he meant. The whole reason for our marriage was for my protection, whether I wanted it or not. And Marco took that seriously. He always had. When I didn't respond, he put more space between us as he moved toward the doorway.

"There are clothes you can change into in the closet. Sofia

stocked everything you should need. I'll meet you downstairs. Take your time."

When the door clicked shut behind him, I spun around carefully, taking in everything. I felt like a damaged modern-day Cinderella. I made my way to the walk-in closet, which was a room in itself. There was an ottoman in the center where I could sit if I chose. There were sets of drawers, tons of shoes in individual cubbies, and rows of clothes—so many. One side was all mine, and along the back, on the opposite wall, were Marco's things. I was a little surprised we were sharing the closet, but there was so much room that I guessed it made sense.

With care, I unzipped then stepped out of the gorgeous wedding gown and hung it on a hanger on a small rod nearest the door. Maybe that was where I would put the clothing that needed laundering.

I selected pants and a cashmere sweater. After slipping on a pair of black ballet flats—no heels for me until my leg was better—I left the bedroom and went in search of Marco. I took the back stairs with a tight grip on the railing. The ache in my leg was constant, but it could have been so much worse. It would heal. I wasn't overly worried. Maintaining movement was important and helped to get the blood flowing to the internal part of the injury. The faster I healed, the closer I would be to my date with the hot tub.

CHAPTER NINE

ELENA

It didn't take long to find everyone—I followed the voices to the main living room off the dining room. I could see the table set from where I stood. I guess we were having a celebratory lunch, as our wedding was basically at breakfast, and only a little time had passed. I was hungry, though.

"Elena!" Sofia screamed then barreled for me. I braced myself for impact, but Marco caught her by the waist then whispered in her ear before letting her go. Her mouth formed an O, and then she was in front of me, carefully wrapping me in her embrace. She was the shortest of all of us, but I swore she had the biggest personality. "I didn't know you were hurt." Then she glared at Marco. "Why did my friend get shot?"

God, I loved her. Marco flinched very slightly, but I wouldn't have noticed it if I hadn't been paying close attention. Sofia was just that fierce. She wasn't often truly mad, so her brothers knew better than to push her. When she was really angry... they'd learned to take cover or appease the monster as quickly as they could.

"I'm fine. I swear."

Sofia turned back to me, her amber eyes narrowing. "Why

did this happen when Marco was there and he doesn't have a scratch on him?"

"He wasn't there. I was running from him, and he came into the alley just as the hit man shot me. Marco killed him. I'm good. Promise."

Sofia shot Marco another glare before letting it go. "He showed me the pictures from this morning." Tears misted her eyes. "You looked so beautiful. I'm still mad we couldn't all be there, but the guys were cavemen. It's like they don't realize we can shoot a gun just as well as they can." She rolled her eyes, and someone else snorted.

I grabbed her hand and squeezed. I'd missed her. "Thank you. For the dress. It's beautiful." I swept my gaze around the room to find Enzo, probably the one who'd snorted. He came over, hugged me, then tucked Sofia into his side, where she obviously fit perfectly. *Those two...* "I'm so happy for you guys." They were meant for each other.

The doorbell rang, and Marco went to see who was there. When he opened the door, a bunch of people must have entered, because the noise level swelled. I transferred my weight to my toes, a habit I had when I wasn't sure if I needed to run or not.

When Lil's platinum hair came into view, I relaxed. Her searching gaze landed on me, and her smile was blinding. I took in how her arm looped through Max's. And the confidence she had... it was clear in the way she walked into the room, the brightness in her eyes, and her carriage in general. I didn't think I'd ever seen her like that before. Living under her father's roof had been tough on her. It was obvious that being with Max was the right move. Maybe I would give him a chance as my new brother.

Next to enter were Emiliana and Stefano. I'd never had much interaction with him, but I'd known how Emiliana felt. It was nice to see them together. Marco's brothers, Trey and Nico, followed them. Tony was next, and then, of course, my mama.

My brows rose when I saw Tony. I never thought he would want to see me, as our relationship in the past had been rocky at best. I shot another peek at Max. *Could this be his doing?*

I said hi to my brother but little else as Mama, Em, Lil, and Sofia absconded to the cozy seating area in front of the fireplace with me. Marco brought wine, then Sofia shooed him away with a parting explanation: "It's our turn to have El all to ourselves. You've monopolized her for the past two days and agreed with our husbands to bar us from her wedding. You're still on my shit list, brother."

Marco rolled his eyes at Sofia, and she bared her teeth. But I caught the sparkle. She may have been mad, but I knew her, and she'd already forgiven him.

Before Marco left us to chat, he dropped a kiss on my cheek. I should have turned my head. *Next time.* My gaze followed him as he walked away. I didn't know what to do about the way he was treating me. It was so foreign to how I remembered things and made me want to shake things up, maybe pull a prank on him to equally rattle him for old times' sake.

"Now that we have you all to ourselves"—Emiliana leaned forward—"what is going on with you two? Is everything good?"

"It looked good from where I'm sitting," Lil said with a wink.

"Gross." Sofia fake gagged, while Mama laughed. "We're *not* talking about my brother right now. There's a ton of things El doesn't know."

"You're caught up with who married who—Stefano and Em, Max and me, and obviously, Sof and Enzo." Lil waved her hand to include everyone. "But did you know that Stefano is the capo now?"

I nodded, impressed. "That had to be an interesting development." The capo was the boss of all bosses. "So he governs the Five Families?"

"Yep." Em popped the P. "It was a pretty epic move. There was a commission and—"

"Em!" Stefano motioned for her to come over. He held a curved sword, and her mouth dropped open. She jumped up then seemed to remember she was talking about something. "It was a small bloodbath, I guess. Be right back."

Sofia snickered. "Yeah, so if we want to leave town, it has to be cleared through Stefano."

"What's going on with your family, Lil? Max is running it?"

"Yeah." She smiled, and her light eyes sparkled. "Maybe not for too long, though."

"The family has changed," Mama said, "definitely for the better." Then her gaze met Sofia's and Lil's as Em headed back to us. "And some not as happy as an ending."

"Like Marissa," Sofia said.

My stomach sank at the mention of our friend. "What happened to her? Marco mentioned she died almost a year ago and that everybody thinks it was the Russians."

"It was Ivan. Do you remember him?"

I shook my head. Of course I knew about him, but our paths —*thankfully*—had never crossed. "Should I?"

Sofia frowned. "I don't think we met him until our last year in college. So no, I don't see how you could have."

"Tell me what happened to Marissa." I leaned over and flicked the switch for the fireplace, and it roared to life. Lil grabbed the wine that Marco had brought and poured it into glasses for us.

Once we all had a glass, Lil spoke. "She was engaged to Tony."

"My brother?" *Wow.* I had no idea. "An arranged marriage or by choice?" I knew they had been friends, but I couldn't see them together.

"Arranged marriage," Emiliana said. "We thought Tony killed her in a fit of rage because Marissa was flirting with Ivan. Sorry, Nicole." Em flinched then glanced at Mama, who waved away her concern. "Marissa didn't always make the best decisions."

"Yeah, well, she paid for it in the end," Sofia murmured.

"On second thought, do we need to dive into all this heavy stuff on the day Elena got married?" Lil asked. "I, for one, would much rather hear about what you've been doing while you were away."

I grinned, happy for the lighter topic. I wanted to know all about what had happened, but maybe not immediately. "I went to college, and when I was there, I became friends with someone who started a security business. I helped him—off the record, of course—test that his designs were sound."

"I'm not surprised." Emiliana laughed. "You had a knack for getting in and out of places. I remember you tormenting Marco by sneaking some of his stuff from his room when he pissed you off."

"Which was often." Sofia giggled. "That was the best entertainment."

I shared a look with Mama, and we both grinned because she knew how I did what I did.

We joked around for another hour, and I told them about living in Hoboken, working at the bookstore, and my night job breaking and entering to test Danny's security systems.

I couldn't have been happier to be back among my friends. Everyone stayed for lunch, and when it was time for them to go, I curled up on the couch in front of the fire, feeling safe and loved, then fell asleep while Marco made work calls nearby.

CHAPTER TEN

MARCO

Sofia and Enzo had hung back and were the last to leave our mini wedding reception. Elena had said her goodbyes and thought they had gone as she curled up on the couch and fell asleep.

I motioned for my sister and Enzo to enter my office, which wasn't far from the entrance. We walked down the hall, and I pushed open the door. Once inside, we sat in the armchairs evenly spaced around the coffee table at one end of the room.

"What is going on with you and Elena?" Sofia crossed her arms over her chest, and Enzo flashed me a grin. "One minute, you're kissing her cheek, and the next, you're glaring at her like it's because of her the Russians are in our lives at all, when you know that's not true."

"It is her fault. At least to some degree." My temper flared to eclipse hers, and my body tensed. "Ivan fucking tortured you to find out where she was."

"You need to get over that," she snapped. "I'm fine. I handled the time spent with him and don't have any lasting issues. Right, Enzo?"

He held his hands up. "Don't pull me into this, Sof. I'm never going to be okay with what happened. But"—he turned to me—"I don't blame Elena for Ivan's actions. The fault was firmly at his feet, and if he wasn't dead, I would hunt him to make sure he breathed his last breath in agony for what he did."

"See?"

Sof stood, leaning over me—at least, she tried. She wasn't that tall. "Stop being so overprotective. I'm fine. I don't know how many times I have to tell you that." She sighed then fell back into her seat. "I know you love me, and I'm fortunate to have three very protective older brothers, but you're married now, and you need to think of El as your partner, not your enemy. This isn't something of her choosing. They killed her mother and have been hunting her ever since. She's more damaged by them than I ever will be."

"Goddammit, Sof." I stood and pulled her in for a hug. "I'd never been so scared in my life as when he had you." She was my baby sister and sometimes a pain in the ass, but our whole family loved her like crazy and was firmly wrapped around her little pinky. When I released her and retook my seat, I didn't miss how Enzo grasped her hand in his. The discussion was way too emotional, but I was glad he was there for her, keeping her safe twenty-four seven. He was the only one I would have trusted to do so.

"There's another issue that's bothering him, Sof." Enzo's voice was gentle. "It's not just the nightmare for us when Ivan had you. It's who will come next. We're all worried about the Bratva and the collateral damage they plan to inflict."

I scrubbed my hands over my face, the worry exhausting me all over again. We were going to war—not that we weren't already there with the Russians—and I felt the intensity of it infuse my bones. When they attacked next, more would die. It was why we hadn't let any of the girls go to the wedding. The Russians could have planned a strategic attack right before we said "I do."

"We have to find out why they want her so badly"—I held my hand up to stop Sofia from stating the obvious—"aside from their grievances over whatever crime her birth mother committed against them."

"That's easy. We have two sources we can go to."

"No," Enzo barked at Sofia. "You're not contacting her."

"I agree with Enzo. There is no way in hell you're establishing another connection with Katya." That was playing Russian roulette. The Bratva assassin was too dangerous. The last thing either Enzo or I wanted was Sofia talking with their angel of death again.

"We'll go with the other option, then, for now." She narrowed her eyes. "Nicole. And I think it should be Elena who asks her, not any of us."

"Why would we do that?" Even though I had feelings for Elena, I had a hard time letting go of my anger. It was a dual-edged sword. I wanted to trust her, but my intuition screamed that there was more to her story, and I didn't know what. Sofia was right. Nicole was the gatekeeper of secrets. If anyone knew why they were after El, and if it was more than the Russians' order to kill everyone in El's mother's family, Nicole would know. It was time to find out.

"If you want this marriage to work, you're going to have to trust El," Enzo said.

Well shit. "Okay. I'll talk to El, and she can go to Nicole if Max is there. And no contacting Katya." I addressed my sister. "She could be the next one they send."

"That wouldn't make sense because she was the one who helped hide El." Sofia frowned then crossed her arms. "We'll have to contact her at some point. Why not now?"

"Because we're going to Nicole first. And I can't figure out why the Bratva's assassin would aid us, the Italians. Think about it, Sof."

"I don't know why she's helping us, but she is. She was the

one who told us where to find Emiliana when the traffickers took her. And she was also the one to help us hide El before anything could happen to her."

"That's the thing, though, Sof." Enzo drew her attention. "Why would a Russian assassin, the freaking angel of death, work with the Italians? She's Bratva. It doesn't make sense."

Sofia shrugged. "I don't know. Maybe things aren't all that good for her with the Bratva. Maybe she wants to defect?"

I grinned at Enzo. That would be a major win on our part. Katya was deadly, possibly more so than all of us put together. "If we uncover her true motivation, it's something to contemplate even though none of us want to work with a former Bratva member or a Russian. Crazy vodka-drinking lunatics."

Sofia snickered, and Enzo grinned before agreeing with me. "It's something to consider. And on that note, Sofia and I are going to go. You need to figure out how to make things work with El. There was always something between the two of you. Now is your opportunity to find out how deep your feelings go and to establish trust rather than cause further damage."

"I can't believe I let you marry my sister." Enzo was a pain in my ass, but truth be told, I wouldn't have been okay with anyone else marrying her. And he knew it.

I walked my sister and Enzo out, making sure to thank her again for everything she did for El, from the gorgeous wedding dress to the closet full of clothes. Having a fashion designer in the family was not without its benefits. Of course, I could have had a personal shopper do everything, but I knew having Sofia select and design her dress would mean more to Elena. And she wouldn't have rejected what had been provided for her.

It was time to talk to El without my defenses interfering.

I stopped in front of the couch where El slept. In sleep, she was soft and approachable, easily one of the most beautiful women I'd ever seen. But awake, her sharp wit and fight-or-flight defenses were in play. I needed her to keep her guard down and let me in. The only way to accomplish that was to do the same because I wanted this relationship to work. She was the only woman I'd ever dreamed of marrying—she just didn't know it.

A sixth sense that she was being watched must have woken her, because her long eyelashes fluttered open. I sat by her feet on the couch, and she tilted her head down to observe me.

"How are you doing?" I rested my hand on her sock-clad foot. She'd kicked off her flats before curling up to nap.

"Adjusting." With her hand flat on the cushion, she flinched as she pushed herself up then scooted to the corner of the couch and stretched her legs out in front of her, still within reach of my hand. "It's so good to see everyone, but I'm worried about what the risks are with my being here. I don't want them to get hurt."

I couldn't help but grin. "We're the Mafia. Aside from my issues about what happened to Sofia, that's inevitable with this life."

"Yeah, but I was out of it for a long time. It's strange being back. I missed a lot, but it's also like I never left."

I moved closer, lifting her legs then rested them across my lap. She didn't protest, which I took as a good sign. "We need to get to the bottom of why you're on the Bratva's list." She opened her mouth, but I held up my finger. "Hold on. I know how they operate, too, but Yuri sent his underboss to do a hit that shouldn't have warranted that. Let's assume there's more to the story behind why they're so intent on having you killed."

"I agree. It seems excessive." She tucked her hair behind her ears. "Then add Katya into the mix and why she would warn me, and it gets even crazier."

"Right. So we have a couple of options to consider gaining additional insight into what could be going on. Nicole is my first choice of who to ask. There's a very small possibility that Stefano could reach out to his oldest sister, Camila." She was married to Vic, the only remaining son of the Bratva boss. "Or Katya. I'd rather not contact her, as she's a wild card, and that could backfire."

"I agree. Let's ask Nicole."

"As long as Max is there, I'm fine with dropping you off at her house for breakfast. That way, you can spend time alone with her. What do you think?"

El smiled then nodded. The world spun on its axis for a moment. I wouldn't admit it to Sofia or Enzo, but they were right. I had to show her trust and partnership rather than blaming her for what had transpired in the past.

She was one of a kind, and if she let me in, I would give her the world.

CHAPTER ELEVEN

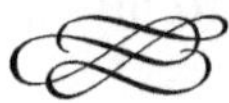

ELENA

arco and I had spent a quiet evening together, eating dinner and watching movies at home. He kept the conversation light, not pressing me for details about the years I was absent from the Mafia. The reprieve, along with his idea that I talk with Mama alone, went a long way toward softening how I felt about him and our marriage of convenience.

We'd slept in the same bed, but he'd kept his word and didn't make any advances toward me. *Am I ready for that?* Whether I was or not, my body had its own plans. I'd fallen asleep hugging the edge of the bed, not wanting to tempt myself. But I'd woken to find myself sprawled across his expansive chest with his arms holding me close. My only consolation was that I wasn't drooling.

He hadn't made a big deal of it, and when I got up to go to the bathroom and brush my teeth—aka hide—he went to make coffee. After showering, I meandered to the kitchen and sat at the island, where Marco had a mug waiting for me with the perfect amount of cream—*heaven*. He must have showered in another room because his hair was damp, and he was dressed for the day in black pants and a dark-gray button-down that molded to him. Secured to his chest in his shoulder harness were his ever-present guns. He slipped a black jacket over them.

The way his hair fell in a wave across his forehead caused my fingers to itch to push it back. It was impossible not to be attracted to him, as he was so handsome. I took my first sip of coffee, needing something to do. He leaned a hip against the counter. My gaze dropped to my mug, but I could feel his eyes on me. *Why am I so nervous?*

"We should be at Nicole's in the next half hour. Max texted that he's already there. Are you ready to go?"

"Mm. Yeah, I have to grab shoes, and then I am." I took a few more sips before I hopped off the barstool to get them. My leg was feeling a lot better. Still stiff, but that would lessen the more I moved around.

It didn't take long for me to finish getting ready. We left through the garage door off the mudroom in silence, with his hand resting on the small of my back. He guided me to the car, opened the door, and waited until I was inside before rounding to his side and getting in.

"I'll be at my sister's house so that you can have some privacy when you talk with Nicole. Unless you text me to come back sooner, I'll be there in a couple of hours."

Nicole could talk, and it was a reunion of sorts. The wedding had been rushed, and we hadn't had time to catch up at the reception with everyone else there. "That sounds great. My guess is the longer, the better."

He chuckled, and we lapsed into silence. I was still trying to wake up, desperate for another cup of coffee. I should have taken a to-go mug. Lesson learned. My mind wandered as the miles disappeared beneath the car's tires. Things were going well between Marco and me. He wasn't pushy or high-handed, and my guard wasn't up like it used to be. This new version of him was extremely attractive, and I worried about how easy it would be to lose my heart to him. It was concerning because I wasn't sure I would survive if he let me go.

"Elena." Marco rested his hand on mine. "We're here."

"Oh." I snapped out of my head and let the house I'd spent most of my childhood years in come into focus. Security stood stationed by the front door, and as I glanced around, I noted that more were patrolling the grounds. "Does there seem to be a higher-than-usual number of guards?"

"Max added detail because you were coming today."

"And he'll be there?" I wasn't sure how I felt about being there with Max. I'd met him at the wedding and at our place afterwards, but I didn't have a chance to talk to him. I wasn't positive how he viewed me, even though Marco and Lil said he thought of me as a sister.

"Yes, Max is inside. And I believe Tony is stopping by, too, but they'll give you privacy to talk with Nicole."

That was good. I needed time with Mama more than anything. After that, I could probably face getting to know Max and reconnecting with Tony, even though I couldn't imagine having a relationship with him. But my friends had said he'd changed, and he hadn't acted like I'd remembered the day before. I had to keep an open mind about him.

Marco got out of the car, and I waited for him to come around and open my door. I knew he wanted that, and it gave me another few seconds to take some deep breaths before I went inside. He extended his hand to help me up, and I grasped onto him. When I was up and steady on my feet, he released me before his large palm rested on my back, guiding me to the front door. It felt so natural for him to touch me in that way, and I took comfort in the small gesture.

The door flung open, and Mama stood there, a huge smile on her face. She looked softer and so much happier. I stayed by Marco's side as he walked to the door. But once I was within arm's reach, Mama enveloped me in a tight hug, allowing me to smell the floral perfume she'd always worn.

"I'll be back soon," Marco said. "Get inside and lock the door behind you."

I nodded.

"Baby Girl, I've missed you so much," Mama said, letting me back her up enough to shut the door. When she finally released me, she slid the bolt home to secure us inside then pulled me toward the sunroom, where we used to like to hang out. It was bright and cheery and so very unlike the rest of the house. There were lots of plants, and the furniture was inviting, the atmosphere casual and cozy.

As she drew me through the rooms, my jaw dropped at what I was seeing. "It's so different in here." And it was. Gone were the stuffy velvet drapes and somber décor from when I'd last been there at age eighteen. A fresh coat of paint lightened the look and feel. There were still floor-to-ceiling drapes but in the same earthy tone that carried through the rooms. "It's beautiful."

"Yeah." Mama's voice softened. "I made changes when Antonio died. When Max stepped in to lead the family, he made sure that the house and money I should have gotten but that Antonio didn't will to me was mine. Tony and I share it, but he has a place in the city and stays there most of the time." She drew me back into another tight hug. "I missed you so much."

"I missed you, too, Mama." Tears misted my eyes. "I wish I could have warned you better before I left."

She drew back and held me at arms' length. "Don't you say that. I understood what you meant before you left. Those last few hours we spent together, getting into Antonio's wines, were precious to me. All I wanted was for you to be safe."

I swiped a tear that'd escaped my lashes. "I know. And I loved Hoboken. I had a beautiful if small place on the Hudson River. I even finished college."

"Oh, sweetheart, I'm so happy to hear that." She looped her arm with mine, and we continued through the house.

I couldn't believe how much she'd changed or the facelift the house had gotten. "You look so healthy."

We entered the sunroom, which had even more plants and flowers than I remembered. There was coffee, orange juice, scones, a bowl of fresh fruit, and several silver cloches covering dishes on the table. After we sat on the love seat, Mama handed me a plate.

"I thought we could do this instead of sitting in the breakfast nook or at the dining room table."

"I'm glad you did. There's no need for formality." I grinned as she removed the metal dome to reveal eggs, bacon, and French toast. My stomach growled, and I piled the plate with food. I hadn't realized how hungry I was.

Mama poured us coffee and orange juice then set to work adding a few things to her plate. "Tony said he'd come by a little later, and after Max is done with his phone calls, he'll join us too. I hope that's okay?"

I was nervous about reuniting with my brothers in such a small setting. But if they were going to try, then I would too. "Sure, that's fine."

We ate for a few minutes in silence before I broached the subject I'd come to talk about with her. It needed to happen before my brothers crashed our mother-daughter morning. "Mama, what happened to Mom? Why are the Russians after me? It feels like there's something else I don't know. And if anyone would know, it would be you."

"Oh, darlin', I've wanted to talk to you about this for so long, but it was risky with Antonio here and the staff. The walls had ears, and I had to be so careful."

"What's changed besides Antonio being gone?" I wondered whether there were still problems with the staff and security.

"Well, there's a long story about how Max and I came to

trust one another. It's something for another day, though. What matters is that he's fired everyone in our household who disrespected me in the slightest way. Then he made it clear what would happen should they cross me." She blinked away tears, fanning her eyes and looking up to keep them from running. "He empowered me."

I set my plate down then hers before launching myself into her arms. Max had my gratitude as well, and I would trust him based on the changes in Mama—she seemed genuinely happy. All Antonio had ever done was tear her down, belittle her. To him, she was an accessory. I could tell she'd stopped getting plastic surgery. Even her makeup was lighter, and her clothes were different, too, more elegant and less showy. I didn't think she minded the clothes all that much, but the surgeries wore on her. She couldn't have a wrinkle or a single imperfection or he would start on her.

"I was afraid to say it before, but I'm so glad Antonio is gone. You deserve every happiness in life and to feel safe and loved."

Her arms tightened once more before she drew back, her hand resting on my cheek. "Baby Girl, I've always felt cared about where you're concerned. The first time I set my eyes on you after I met your mother sealed the deal. I loved you unconditionally from that moment, and when she asked me to take you in if anything happened to her, there wasn't even a question. I knew I would bend Antonio to my will if something were ever to happen to her. I only wish she didn't have to die for me to be in your life."

"She knew they were coming for her. I remember those last weeks. How jumpy she was, how she'd made me practice hiding, and if I made any noise, I had to do it five more times at random that same day." When Nicole cringed, I rushed to reassure her. "She made a game of it. A part of me was very aware that if I had to hide, it was going to be bad, but she made it sort of fun, and we had ice cream at the end of the day, and she'd tell me how amazing I was." I grinned. "I was motivated for the ice cream."

"Daniela had that playful quality about her, even when things were bad. Her resourcefulness... well, that was something we had in common and bonded over from the start." Nicole shook her head, and her honey-blond hair spilled over her shoulder. I liked the new color. It was more natural than platinum.

"My mother taught me many things but always made a game of it. Pickpocketing and how to get out of zip ties were only two. She started my martial arts training. Then after she passed, you made sure I was even more prepared." I covered her hand with mine. "Thank you for that. But Mama, I need to know why the Russians want me dead, and I have a feeling it's for much more than just being related to her."

"You're a lot like her in appearance. Daniela had this compelling and effervescent quality that drew men to her. It was something Frank Rossi extorted."

"Don't you mean Antonio?"

Mama flinched ever so slightly, and my sense of unease spiked.

"No. She worked for Frank at first. I didn't learn this until later. The first time I met Daniela was in this house, in the library. It was late at night, and she'd slipped past a guard that was told to let her through. Once inside, she left coded notes in the spine of a book. She was working for Frank as a spy against the Bratva. Antonio recruited her to share information with him for an exorbitant amount of money. As a bonus, she was to tell him anything she'd learned about Frank."

"I don't... what does that mean? If she was working for Frank first, then—"

"She was a distant cousin in the Rossi family."

My world spun. Nothing made sense. "Then I'm a Rossi?" My voice rose in pitch.

Mama took my hands in hers and squeezed, her gaze locking on mine with the precision of a drill sergeant. "No. You're a Caruso. Well, now that you're married, you're a La Rosa. But nothing about you is different. From the moment you entered this household, you were my daughter."

I held onto her like a lifeline. I needed to rip the Band-Aid off and hear it all. "Please tell me the rest. What else did you learn about my mother from Antonio?"

Mama sucked in a breath then let it out slowly. "Daniela was a spy. And for a year and a half, she lived among the Pavlov Bratva. I don't know what secrets she found out—I never could get that out of Antonio—but I do know that she had to get out of the Pavlov empire fast."

Mama waited a second, her eyes narrowing, assessing, before she decided I was ready to hear more. "Frank was a cold son of a bitch. Camila was a peace offering he married off to the Pavlov family to stop their attack against him for inserting Daniela into their household."

"Why did my mother ask you to take me in? Why didn't someone in the Rossi family do it instead?"

"Daniela didn't trust Frank not to hand you over to the Pavlov Bratva. And I didn't either."

I pulled my hands free and rubbed my eyes. My mind was spinning in a thousand directions. "How long did you know her?"

"Only for a few short months before she was killed. Most of the information, I pried out of Antonio, and some from Daniela. I'm sorry, sweetheart. But that's all I know."

The memories of how she died roared to life, starting with the crash as the Russian soldiers broke down the door. She'd cried out. I'd wanted to go to her so badly, but it had been ingrained in me to hide in the one place she'd had me rehearse repeatedly. My body was on auto, relying on the muscle memory of what to do if I heard the sounds she'd played on a recording so I wouldn't be surprised and react. And I did. It was what saved my life, just as she'd planned. When I was safely in the hollowed-out bottom of the kitchen cabinet with the door shut and the basket that she'd stuck to the plywood with what appeared to be one of the detergents tipping over, I heard the gunshot.

Men riffled through the place, and I lay there with my hand pressed over my mouth and silent tears running down my face. I didn't even know how long I stayed. Finally, there were other sounds, different men walking through the space. I didn't move a muscle. I'd promised her I wouldn't. Mama—Nicole—had found me. When she removed the panel, mascara streaked her cheeks, and she'd cried out when she saw me. She lifted me out and wrapped me tightly in her arms then covered my eyes and took me out of our home and into a waiting car. That was the last time I'd ever seen the home I'd lived in with my mother.

"El. Are you okay, honey?" Mama had my hands securely in hers, concern swimming in her light-blue eyes.

"I'm fine. Just remembering." I shouldn't have been surprised by the information. My mother had taught me all those skills I'd used on Marco when we were younger. It was a shock, regardless, and I waited to hear what else Mama had to say.

"She came out of Russia hot, and from what she told me, your father was the one to help her escape the Bratva. He was killed months after he'd gotten her to safety in the States."

I'd heard about my father dying before I was born and that he was a soldier, a made man not related to the Caruso family by blood.

It shouldn't have surprised me that my mother had been a spy. "So the Bratva thinks I know something? Is that why they're after me so hard?"

She shrugged. "I don't know for sure. Max has been poring over Antonio's records, both digital and on paper. He hasn't found much about Daniela. It could be as simple as you being a loose end. I didn't think they knew about you. She was always so careful. But they'd been in your home, and there was no mistaking child-sized clothes or toys. She always kept any pictures of you in a lockbox hidden in another hollowed-out cabinet in the home you shared."

"The photo albums you had in my room here."

"Yes. I took them so I could make those for you. You needed something of her, and it was the least I could do." She inhaled a shuddering breath. "That day at the park, they'd found you."

She meant the day I was shot and Alfonso Rossi, brother to Marissa, Camila, and Stefano, was killed. His blood had spread across my body, intermixing with mine, to give the impression that their mission had been accomplished.

I nodded my understanding. Mama and I were on the same page with our thoughts, the guilt we shared curving in her shoulders. It was a terrible price to pay to stay hidden from the Bratva.

CHAPTER TWELVE

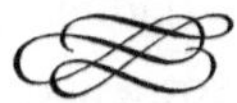

ELENA

Our breakfast was long since cold. Mama and I wiped our eyes and were ready to put the past behind us. After the heavy discussion about my birth mother's history, we moved on to what Mama had been doing and what I thought about my marriage to Marco, and she was relentless. I couldn't get her to drop it.

"You had such a crush on Marco when you were younger. The arranged marriage—I thought it was a solid solution to keeping you safe."

"It's weird because of how Marco and I were married. I know he'll do everything in his power to protect me. That's how he is. It's the rest that makes me uncomfortable." *Specifically sex with him.*

A wicked grin spread across Mama's face, and her eyes sparkled mischievously. "Things will work out. Trust me. He's just as taken with you as you are with him."

She was crazy. I rolled my eyes in answer, but her expression returned to the serious one before, and the fine hairs on the back of my neck stood at attention.

"There's something else, El," she said just as Max and Tony

walked into the sunroom, eclipsing the light. She gave a small shake of her head, and I did the best I could to hide my anxiety about whatever she was about to tell me but couldn't with the guys walking in.

I shifted my gaze to Tony, who resembled Mama so much with his light-brown hair and heart-shaped face. Oddly, it didn't look feminine on him. He had a rakish quality that I could imagine being appealing to some women.

Max was over six feet tall with broad shoulders. His dark hair was short, and his five o'clock shadow only accented his unusual gray eyes.

"Hey, El. Glad you're alive." Tony bent down and kissed my cheek.

I grinned because it was so strange. We'd barely acknowledged each other in the past. "Hi, Tony." Then my gaze went to Max. "Max." For him, my smile was a tad more genuine because of everything he'd done for Mama.

"I hope you don't mind us crashing your breakfast," Max said while Tony grinned, helping himself to a scone and coffee.

"You boys are always welcome." Mama graciously waved them to dig in to whatever was left. "Do you want me to ask Melanie to bring anything else?"

Melanie was Mama's favorite staff member, the one who'd stood up against a few of the others in the household when they'd subtly snubbed her. I assumed they were gone now. Since Mel was the only one Mama trusted, she helped out by being a nanny to me. That became Mel's primary responsibility if Mama had something to do with Antonio, who would not have understood the necessity of ballet lessons, mixed martial arts class, or even bedtime stories.

"How are you doing, Tony, after your dad's death?" I probably shouldn't have asked, especially because of the circumstances around how he was killed and by whom.

He set his plate down and scrubbed his face with his hands

for a minute. "I'm good now. But it took me a while to get here. There was no pleasing Dad, and I was still in the same unhealthy, driven mindset for a while after Max got here. I'm managing the clubs now." A genuine smile curved his lips. "It's what I was meant to do. I'm happy. You and Marco should come by sometime."

Max cleared his throat. "When things have calmed down."

Tony's eyes widened. "Shit, yeah. I wasn't thinking."

I waved away his apology. His stricken expression went a long way toward me wanting to give him a chance. It would be nice to build a relationship with him and Max.

"Where's Lil?" I asked Max. For some reason, I'd thought she would be there with him.

"She didn't want to intrude on your first time alone with Nicole. She's doing something with Emiliana. We'll all be together soon. At the very least, we have family dinners every Sunday at Emiliana and Stefano's place. If you don't see Lil before, you will then."

"That sounds like fun. I'm sure Marco and I will be there."

Mama was keeping quiet, letting the boys talk to me at their own pace. For that reason, silence descended on us for a few awkward seconds until Tony spoke. "I'm sorry about all the crap when we were growing up. I had Dad in my head, trying to mold me into some skewed version of himself. Things have changed, and I'd like to get to know you for real, not like before."

I grinned because we didn't know each other before. He'd avoided me and ignored me as much as he could. "I'd like that, Tony."

My phone pinged with a text from Marco, who was on his way. Part of me was glad to escape the awkwardness of finding something to talk about with my brothers, but I also didn't want my time with Mama cut short. She must have sensed it because she pulled me in for one of her famous hugs, the kind she reserved just for me. I always felt like everything was right in my world, no matter how wrong things really were, when she held me like that.

"We'll get together soon. Maybe have our visit in the library next time." She tucked a strand of hair behind my ear, a soft smile curving her lips. "Remember what I said about you and Marco."

I felt heat stain my cheeks at her reference to Marco and our marriage working itself out. Then her mention of the library registered. It was code that only the two of us would have understood. Later, when we were alone again, I would do as she'd suggested and visit the library. Maybe whatever she'd wanted to share would be hidden away in the spine of one of the books there. It'd been a long time since I'd been in the library, and I wondered what I would find.

But Mama had said Max was looking into Antonio's records too. I snuck a glance at him, wondering whether he knew that Mama and I liked to leave coded messages for one another in the library, or if he'd known about the ones my mother had left for Antonio about Frank and the Bratva.

I nodded, unable to speak past the lump in my throat. She always knew what was going through my head. And she was right. It was time that I gave my relationship with the boy I'd had a crush on who'd become the man I was discovering even more about a chance. Because I didn't want a marriage of convenience—I wanted it all.

CHAPTER THIRTEEN

ELENA

Marco came into the house to get me. I gave Mama another long hug and a quick one to each of my brothers before going with my new husband to the car. He seemed to sense my melancholic mood and didn't press for information.

Mama bringing up the library was running through my mind, tugging me back in time. I rested my head against the headrest and closed my eyes, following the memories until I was once again a little girl playing a game that only the two of us knew.

On quiet feet, I crept into the vast room with floor-to-ceiling bookshelves, sliding ladders, and comfortable chairs with softly glowing lights beside them. Several blankets were thrown over the backs to snuggle under with a good book. I could spend hours in there without anyone but Mama or Mel finding me. It was also where I discovered the first note.

It was late, and I was supposed to be in bed when I went into the library. Mama was home, which always made me feel better. I had been living there for a little over a year, and on the nights she had to go out with Antonio, I liked to go there, where I felt safest. But that night, even though she was home, I couldn't sleep. Mama never got mad at me when she found me in there, and no one else caught me because I was careful not to make noise.

I stood before one of the bookcases. There was a small section with books that a child would like. They were for me. But instead of taking a couple from my shelf, the red leather ones on the other wall drew my notice. I went over to them and ran my fingers across the spines, something I had done before, probably because in my old home with Mom, she had a similar book. But that time, when I touched them, something felt different. I couldn't tell what. I did it again until I could figure it out. The bloodred book fifth from the end was thicker in the way the leather stretched across the back of the spine and pushed out a tiny bit. I wouldn't have noticed if I hadn't been touching it.

With a quick peek over my shoulder, I checked to make sure I was alone before removing the heavy book then lugging it over to the side table next to my favorite chair. I flipped through the pages once then again. I didn't notice anything unusual, so I stood it up, fanning the inside open so the spine bulged a little. A small note was tucked between the leather and the pages' binding.

Mama walked in, and I set the book back down before I had a chance to look at what was hidden inside.

"A little light reading, Baby Girl?" She dropped to her knees in front of my chair and hugged me to her. I relaxed because I knew she wouldn't be mad. I smothered a yawn against her shoulder, and she laughed.

"Let's get you to bed." She returned the book to where it was then took my hand and led me to my room. After she tucked me back into bed with a kiss on my forehead, she bopped my nose. "Always make sure that book is back where you found it, my sweet."

She'd never told me I couldn't look at it, and the next time I was in the library alone, I did, and I found a secret note. And there were others, but those were ones that Mama left for me. They were coded, but I knew what they said because my mom played games with me where we would write in a way that used the alphabet differently. I would have to count the letters then copy the correct sequence. I'd learned the code as soon as she taught me to read and write. I was reading full-length sentences at three years old, and by the time I was four, we'd started playing the secret code game. By seven, I could do the codes in my sleep.

I'd never questioned how Mama knew them too. I should have. Maybe one day, I would.

I blinked and pulled myself out of the past when Marco parked the car in our garage. Usually, he left it in the driveway, and one of the guards would move it in later. Instead, though, we entered through the door connecting the garage to the house. The garage was massive, and he had at least ten cars inside. I was tired and stressed about what I'd learned that morning. It felt like the day should be over, but it was only early afternoon.

"You were lost in thought the whole way home. Are you okay?"

"Yeah, just thinking about everything."

The understanding way he squeezed my hand settled my thoughts even more, and I smiled back at him before he got out and rounded the car to my side. We walked through the garage, and I glanced outside as the door automatically shut, blocking out the dismal fall day.

The biting chill to the overcast day only added to my exhaustion. I could have used a nap or some pampering. The feeling of Marco's hand at my back as we walked into the house was comforting, and I drew from his strength.

"Glass of wine?"

The deep cadence of his voice made me want to lean into him, which surprised me a little. I'd dropped my guard, mainly because of the olive branch he'd offered by letting me have space and supporting me through my process of figuring things out.

"Wine sounds great. Thanks." I kicked off my shoes and sat on the couch, tucking my legs under me. It didn't take long until he returned with a glass of red for each of us.

He extended his arm over the back of the couch, his fingers playing with the ends of my hair as we sipped in silence. The light touch was soothing and made it easier for me to feel connected to him and open up about what I'd learned.

"My birth mother was a spy for Frank Rossi, planted in the Pavlov Bratva. And she reported to Antonio Caruso behind Frank's back." I went into the details that Mama had shared with me, including my lineage, the games we would play, and the worst-case-scenario drill she had me do until it became muscle memory and ultimately saved my life.

"It makes more sense, then, how vigilant they are about going after you. The first time you were assumed dead should have ended things. But if they think you have something of Daniela's that's vital to them, I can see the driving force behind their actions." He dropped his hand to my shoulder. "How are you feeling about learning your mother was a spy?"

Tears sprang to my eyes, and I pressed my lips together, horrified by my emotional reaction. *Why is this a big deal? We're in the Mafia. Danger is commonplace.* I took a deep breath, trying to make sense of my thoughts. Marco pulled me against his side, and I lost it.

My body shook, and he took the wineglass from my hand, set it down, then drew me into his embrace. The heat from his chest beneath my damp cheek helped me feel less alone. There had been so many changes lately, and I wasn't coping well.

"It's a lot to take in." His hand rubbed slow, mesmerizing

circles on my back, and he pressed a kiss to the top of my head. "But at least we know what's motivating the Russians where you're concerned. I'll make sure Max knows... or you would rather tell him yourself?"

"It doesn't matter. You can tell Max." What was important was that he'd considered that I might want to talk to Max myself. "The things my mom and I used to do, the games and the hiding drill... it all makes sense now. I feel like she was training me."

He tucked a stand of hair behind my ear, his fingers tailing along my neck before he buried his hand in my hair. I shivered from the boldness of his touch. "I'm sure she was. But she was smart to set up contingency plans for your care if anything happened to her. She loved you very much."

That brought me to the next topic I wanted to cover. "She did, and that's not something I'm questioning. I think I'm overwhelmed with it all at the moment. But there's something else that's bothered me, and I think we should talk about it." I wanted to keep my face pressed against his chest, cuddled in the safety of his embrace. That wasn't the best way to have an honest discussion, though. I put my hand flat on his chest and applied a little pressure until he released me.

His gaze dropped to my lips. "What is it?"

Once his hooded eyes locked back on mine, I dropped the bomb. "I don't want a marriage of convenience. I want it all, one that's real, with you."

CHAPTER FOURTEEN

MARCO

Everything in me stilled when Elena said she wanted a real marriage with me. It was the last thing I expected to hear, especially since we'd had such a rocky start when I found her in New Jersey.

"Where is this coming from? Why the change of heart?" Probably not the best questions, but I wanted to make sure she wasn't just reacting to finding out her biological mom was a former spy who'd lived among the Pavlov family, the very people trying to kill her.

"I want what Sofia, Lil, and Emiliana have. I've seen how happy my friends are." She shrugged as if it wasn't a big deal. But the slight tremble to her full lower lip told me otherwise.

"I'm open to a real relationship. We should talk more, though." I wanted to hash a few things out soon. If we didn't, the past would bite us in the ass and set us back. It wasn't something I wanted to risk. "I need to make that call to Max to tell him what you told me, on the off chance he doesn't already know. Why don't you get changed, and we can talk in the hot tub? There are waterproof bandages in the bathroom you can put over your wounds."

"Okay." She pushed off the couch and made her way to our bedroom.

Our drinks were on the end table. I took the glasses to the kitchen, topped them off, then took them outside so I could take the cover off of the hot tub and turn on the jets. Once it was set up, I moved the wine within easy reach then went back inside to call Max.

He answered on the second ring. I didn't bother to say it was me. He had caller ID. "Did you know about Daniela Caruso spying in the Bratva for Antonio?"

"No. Not until after Elena left. Nicole felt she should be the first to learn about what her mother did for the family."

"This changes things." Our war with the Pavlov Bratva was heating up. We had had to be careful so various people wouldn't get caught in the crossfire, including Stefano's sister, Camila, but I wasn't sure how to avoid that.

"It does. We need to have a meeting. I'll call the rest of the bosses, and we'll set something up for late tonight. I'll text you the details."

I agreed that was the best course of action, and we hung up as El walked from the bedroom to where the hot tub was outside. She had on a red silk robe, and her feet were bare. I stood frozen as she slipped the cover from her shoulders and dropped it to a chair. A bikini that matched her robe hugged her curves, and my mouth went dry. I needed to get my ass out there. In long strides, I went to the bedroom and quickly changed into board shorts. I didn't bother with anything else.

By the time I pulled the sliding glass doors open and stepped outside, El was submerged up to her neck in the bubbling water. It didn't matter. The image of her body was seared into my mind, driving me crazy.

Her gaze followed me, crawling over my body and getting hung up on the tattoos I'd added over the years to my chest and arm.

I set my gun on the ledge, swiped the wineglasses in one hand, and got in beside her so that our thighs were touching. Once I was seated, I offered her a glass. The contrast between the hot water and cold air was as tantalizing as my mental image of her under the water, and I spent a lot of time in there when stressful situations got to be too much. Sharing the experience with El was a game-changer that would only bring us closer.

It was difficult to go slowly with her so close. The image of her red bikini hugging her curves was seared into my mind. The light touch of our thighs only tempted me to run my hands over every inch of her, to feel the softness of her skin, and to lift her so she straddled me. I clenched my hand into a fist to keep from reaching for her, knowing she would reject me. Despite how much I needed to touch her, there was more to what I wanted between us, and part of that was sharing experiences and relaxing together like we were doing. It was time we let the past go, clearing a few things up along the way.

"I never hated you." It needed to be said, so I put it out there.

"Well, you didn't trust me," she countered.

I chuckled because she'd had a hell of a way of testing my limits when we were younger. "The Xbox and some of the other pranks you pulled were frustrating. Not gonna lie. But in a way, it was amusing."

"Wow, I amused you?" Her beautiful eyes were wide, and her lips parted in surprise.

"More like challenged me." I couldn't stop the grin from spreading across my face. The way she tormented me had been genius, giving my sister a run for her money. I didn't think even Sofia could have come up with some of the clever ways El had punished me for being a dick. And I knew my sister helped, but El had been the one pulling the strings.

Her laugh was mischievous, and I wanted to crowd her and cover her lips with mine, but I forced myself to stay where I was. We needed a foundation. She was worth taking things slow.

"Aside from all that, why did you change?" Vulnerability bled through her quiet words. "One day we were good, and the next, you were growling at me, ignoring me, or snapping at me like I was dirt beneath your feet. An annoyance."

I ran a hand over my face, regret running deep. I'd fucked things up back then. I had to try to make her understand. "I was young, and I should have known better. I have a sister. It wasn't like I didn't know how to talk to girls. But there was the added pressure of being groomed to take over our family as boss one day. And the thing about this life was, we never had assurances of when. Dad could have gotten killed the next day, and I would have had to step into his shoes seamlessly. So when I found out that the girl I'd had a crush on forever was promised to someone else, I didn't react well. I'm sorry for that, El."

"I didn't know." She scooted away enough that we faced each other. "They didn't tell me until my junior year in high school. You changed before you were a freshman. I guess you knew long before I did. But that wasn't the only thing. You would watch me with so much mistrust."

She wasn't wrong. I'd always had a sense that there was more to her past than anyone would admit. Even my dad didn't know anything other than that the attack had been by the Russians. There had been some speculation about El, but nothing could be proven. "I couldn't figure out why you and Nicole would dye your hair different colors every few months. The style of clothes you wore would change.

"Then there was the fact that you didn't go out as much as everyone else did. You stayed home when we did group things like going to the lake house in Michigan or sneaking into one of the clubs we owned." We had been underage, but being in the Mafia gave us different rules, and Enzo's family and Antonio's—Max's—owned most of the clubs. "Nicole was always watching you and the surrounding area, when you both were out in public. I knew there was something not safe about you. It was like I was constantly at war with myself. Part of me wanted to protect you. The other half wanted you away from my sister."

"The protect-the-world-against-me side won out." Sadness turned her blue-green eyes stormy.

"Not even close." I tucked a strand of damp hair behind her ear, my fingers trailing over her soft cheek. My hand fell away, but I didn't miss the shiver that traveled over her in the wake of my touch.

"It felt that way, even if you didn't mean it. I had such a crush on you, and when you pushed me away, I didn't know how to deal with it."

"I could have handled things differently back then, but I was a stupid teenager and thought I had to push you away. We have history." I swore my heart skipped a beat when El grinned and her eyes lit up.

"Not the best history."

"It's something to build on. Besides, there were good times. All the chasing was like foreplay, in a way."

She sucked in a breath, and I could tell she wasn't sure what to think.

"The hardest part for me was as we grew, it didn't matter how much I wanted you for myself, even if I thought it was a terrible idea because of your mysterious past. You were never mine to have."

When her eyes softened and her lips parted, I couldn't resist the pull she had over me. I wouldn't push things any further, but it felt right to lean in and kiss her. We needed that connection, and I was fairly sure we both wanted it.

I leaned close, slipping my hand behind her neck to bury my fingers in her hair. I moved slowly to give her a choice to pull back if she wanted. Every muscle in my body tensed in anticipation. At the first brush of our lips, my body ignited. She was so soft and intoxicating. When she parted her lips, something roared inside me, a deep possessiveness I couldn't deny. I loved everything about El—her independence, her intelligence, the crazy way she could change her appearance like a chameleon, and how she felt in my arms.

My fingers tightened in the hair at the nape of her neck, tilting her head for a deeper angle. Her soft moan reverberated through my entire being. I dropped my hands so they fell to her hips and lifted her until she straddled me. Water sloshed around us, the bubbles a frenzy of movement until they settled with our new position.

She held herself up enough so only our chests were touching. I kept my hands on her hips while her arms wrapped around my neck. We stayed just far enough apart that I could maintain some semblance of control and not tear her bikini off and plunge into her as I wanted. I would take things slowly until I knew she was ready.

Time slipped away as I lost myself in how right El felt in my arms. Each touch and taste sent a jolt of intense awareness through me, making it harder to stop, though I needed to. Baby steps. It was important, at least for the time being, no matter how difficult.

I broke the kiss and put some space between us but felt the loss of her immediately. Her gorgeous oceanic eyes were dilated, the molten-gold flecks almost eclipsed by black. Her full, pouty lips were swollen from my kisses, tempting me to taste her again. The wet strands of her hair clung to her neck, where her pulse fluttered erratically.

There was no more denying my feelings for her. As a kid, I'd crushed hard on the mysterious girl who'd snuck into our lives and consumed my mind. And I still didn't know if I could trust her, but in that moment, I couldn't care less. I wanted her. Every part of her. I could deal with our trust issues in the morning. The part of me that held back faded to the background with her suspicious past. I didn't care anymore. She was mine. We would make it work. I loved her.

El cleared her throat then retook her seat next to me. "So… that changes things."

I laughed. She wasn't kidding. I adjusted myself under the water, trying to ease some of the discomfort. "I told you before. I won't pressure you. But I want you, El."

When she turned toward me with wide eyes and her teeth worrying her lower lip, I had to fist my hands to keep from grabbing her and drawing her back onto me.

"I want more. Maybe not tonight, but soon. Next time"—she winked as she got out of the water—"don't stop."

In a flutter of silk, her robe was once again around her, covering her lean but curvy body. I barely registered the sound of my phone ringing on the ledge nearby. It kept on going, and I continued to ignore it. I didn't dare move until she was out of sight, or I was liable to pounce on her. I wanted El like I wanted my next breath.

When my phone rang for the third time, I got out of the hot tub, grabbed a towel, then answered. "What?"

"I got a call from Yuri," Max said by way of a greeting. "He says that Elena is theirs, and they expect us to deliver her."

CHAPTER FIFTEEN

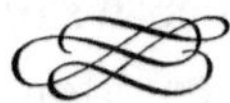

MARCO

There's no way in hell we'd turn El over to the Russians.

The hot tub whirled by my side, water still dripping from my body. I lifted my gun from the ledge where I'd left it, my fingers curling around the handle. Anger sizzled through me so strongly that I didn't feel the cold November air as I hit the button to turn the jets off. I brought my phone back to my ear, my gun securely in my other hand as I scanned my property while waiting for Yuri, the boss of the Pavlov Bratva, to answer.

My men were out there, patrolling the grounds and reporting back to my captain, Tom. After Yuri picked up his goddamned phone, I would update Tom about the threat level—it was much worse than before. They were going to try to take what was mine. Boss or not, I would kill Yuri if he laid a hand on El.

Out of the corner of my eye, I watched El emerge from changing. She stood in the living room, giving me a questioning look through the sliding doors, her gaze dropping to my gun before she went for one of her own. *Fierce. A warrior in her own right.* My chest swelled at the sight of the cold determination stamped across her breathtaking features.

"I expected your call, Marco." Yuri's gruff and heavily accented voice ended the incessant ringing on his end.

"This is my one courtesy to inform you that Elena is my wife. If you go against her, you're taking me on, and you won't like what'll happen."

"She and I have unfinished business. I demand justice for my son Ivan's death. I will end her. It's only fair, a life for a life." His voice shook with anger and emotion.

But Ivan had been a plague. "Ivan was an uncontrollable psychopath. We did you a favor by putting a bullet in his head."

"Say goodbye to those you love, Marco. I'm about to cause you more pain than you can possibly imagine."

After his parting words, Yuri hung up. The chill in his voice complemented my burning need for blood. We were on the same page. There would be no commission called where the bosses in Chicago and Italy convened, no sanctioned kills. He was out for what was mine, and I would end him.

I slid the door open, stepped into the living room, secured the door behind me, then faced El's questioning gaze. "I spoke to Yuri. He's coming for us, but we'll be ready." There was no point in saying he was mainly after her.

"When?"

El followed me into the bedroom as I stripped off my board shorts then quickly dressed, securing two guns in my shoulder holster, one in the waistband of my pants, and the other in my hand. I stashed extra magazines in my pockets. When I looked up from getting ready, El was doing the same. I couldn't help but grin at the sight of her, all badass with weapons and that determined glint in her eyes.

"Seeing you like this makes me think of when you were there for the war games my brothers and Sofia played on the wooded lot."

Laughter spilled from her lips. "Paint guns and traps. I remember them well. Even have a scar or two. Good times."

Then she winked, and how sexy she was made my mind go blank. It took my phone vibrating to snap me out of my stupor. I glanced at the screen before answering. It was Enzo, which reminded me I needed to give my brothers a heads-up too.

"Max called you?" he asked. There was no need for greetings.

We didn't know where Yuri would strike first. It could be my home or against my sister to hurt me and then El, which would break me. "Yeah. How bad is it?"

"Not good."

I set my gun down next to me and rubbed a hand across my forehead before picking it back up. "My guess is he'll target Sofia or our brothers in addition to El. I don't know who will be first. We all need to be on alert."

"I hate this defensive shit."

"I agree. It's much better when we're going after our enemies instead of waiting for them to strike. Any word on where they're staying?" I needed to talk to my captain sooner rather than later.

"No, I haven't heard anything. Sof and I are headed to your parents' house. Trey isn't there yet—he's on shift at the hospital, from what Sofia said—but Nico is leaving the bank and meeting us there."

"Good. Stash her in the panic room. El and I will head there in the next few minutes, and she'll go in there too."

"The hell I will." El stepped in front of me and glared.

Enzo laughed. "You're getting the same reaction I expect from Sof when I tell her. Good luck, man."

"You don't get to tell me what to do, Marco." My sister's voice pierced my ear. Enzo snorted, which made me want to punch him. "I can fight the same as Trey and Nico, something you know well."

I could feel a headache coming on. "It's not about that. Yuri wants retribution for his son, which is you and El. No matter how well you can shoot a gun, you're his top targets. It'll be easier on the rest of us if we know you're safe."

"Sorry, big brother. This is my fight, too, and I'm not hiding."

"Goddammit!" I ground my teeth as Sofia hung up on me. El was still staring me down. I was in for a fight.

"Based on your reaction, she told you to fuck off."

I growled, incapable of forming words that she wouldn't use against me later. I knew the game well and wasn't falling for it with El either. "Stay with me." It was all I could do to remain even a little calm.

I texted Tom to meet me in the living room as I left the bedroom with El on my heels. We needed to beef up security and find out if any intel had come in about where Yuri was staying. It would be better if we hit him first.

The side door slammed, and Tom emerged from the garage then joined us in the kitchen. He was a mountain of a man who had a ninja's ability, which was surprising given his size. It came in handy, though. Best of all, he commanded our soldiers in such a way that they respected him just as much as they feared his wrath—or that he would inform me of their transgression and I would mete out punishment—if they let him down. The only one higher up the ladder for our soldiers were my siblings, with me at the top of the hierarchy as boss of the La Rosa family. Regardless, Tom's role as captain worked in our family quite well.

El and I closed the distance across the large open-concept space and met him at the island.

After I briefed him about the call from Yuri and the stakes, he left to prepare our men, and I led El to the weapons room that I had built to be similar to the one in my parents' house. We stopped before a solid door with a keypad. I punched in the code, and the lock slid open with an audible pop. I swung the door wide, and we entered. Weapons were mounted on all available wall space. Trunks holding magazines and boxes of ammo lined the floor. Tactical gear hung neatly on a rack and stacked on a section of shelving.

I found a Kevlar vest that would fit El. She shook her head, but I wasn't having any of it. "Please do this for me. If you won't go into the panic room with Sofia, then wear this."

She pressed her full lips together but took the vest from me. After taking off her gun holsters, she whipped her long-sleeved black shirt over her head to reveal a sexy lace bra. I got distracted in the swell of her breasts, the curve of her waist, and how much I wanted to strip the rest of her clothes off of her—if only we'd had the time. There wasn't enough, but I could steal a kiss. As she threaded her arms through the vest, I used both halves to pull her close. When I slanted my lips over hers, my world tilted, and everything but how right El felt faded. The softness of her skin, the way her lips moved with mine, her taste, and how readily she responded… nothing else mattered.

I devoured her urgently. When I broke the kiss, we were both panting. I ran my thumb over her kiss-swollen bottom lip, longing for more time with just the two of us. When it was all over, I wanted twenty-four hours with her without interruption.

Our gazes never wavered as I fastened her vest then pressed another kiss to her lips. "Stay by me. Survive, El. I need you." I wanted to tell her more, but it wasn't the time.

"I'm good at surviving. You don't need to worry about me." She squeezed my hand then stepped back. She pulled her shirt over her head to hide the Kevlar then strapped the guns to her body and shoved ammo into her pockets. Good thing she had black cargo pants on, as they had a lot of pockets. A thin strip of her skin showed between the top of her waistband and where her shirt ended. Sexy as hell.

When she turned to pull more weapons from the wall, I did too. I slung an M16 with a laser scope over my shoulder by the strap then another. When we emerged from the weapons room and made our way to the living room, the sun was setting. The days were shorter, and night came too quickly, which meant Yuri would arrive soon if he was headed our way.

"Honey, I'm home!" Trey yelled.

I was surprised he had arrived already. Then Enzo rounded the corner, and I did a double take when I saw Sofia. I had to fight to keep my gun pointed at the ground instead of at him. "You brought my sister here?"

He shook his head as the door slammed, and my brother Nico, Max, Lil, Tony, Stefano, and Emiliana entered. "Have you tried to tell Sof what to do? It was take her here or bring her here. I don't even want to tell you what the other option was." He pushed out a breath then looked at my sister with equal parts admiration and horror. "It wasn't pretty. That's all I'm going to say."

Sofia's sly smile did nothing to ease the new tension forming between my shoulder blades. She rapped her knuckles against El's stomach. "You're wearing a vest?"

"Marco made me." El's head swiveled as she caught sight of Emiliana and the curved blades she wore. "I love those!"

"Thanks. Stefano gave them to me as a gift." She took the karambit swords from their sheaths and twirled them before securing them over her back.

I turned to Stefano, hoping he had what we needed. "Any news on where Yuri is?"

"Not yet, but we'll know soon," he replied. "I have people stationed throughout the city."

Everyone had guns, but there was room for more. I pointed them in the direction of the weapons room so they could add gear, not at all happy that my sister was there. My brothers waltzed in and weaponed up, and while it was great to have everyone as backup, I didn't want to lose anyone I loved.

"It'll be okay." El rested her hand on my chest, and I lifted it to my mouth, pressing a kiss to her palm.

"They would have brought additional security. This place should be crawling with our men, but that doesn't mean casualties won't happen."

"Ready to do this?" Stefano's grin was evil as he took the safety off his Glock. He and Emiliana wore the most weapons.

They were also incredibly vicious, even more than the rest of us, which was saying a lot. It made sense, though, as Stefano was the capo—the boss of the bosses.

We decided who would take what section of the house or grounds then put in earbuds so we could communicate with one another. Then we were off—until an explosion shook the ground beneath our feet.

"El!" Acrid smoke and rubble rained down on us. The hallway that led to our bedroom was gone. Blind panic coursed through me at the thought of her gone too.

CHAPTER SIXTEEN

ELENA

They'd hit us with a rocket launcher. My ears rang, and I stumbled over rubble on the ground. Tears welled as my eyes stung with the smoke. Marco's voice sounded hollow, and it took me a moment to register that he was calling me. "I'm here." I coughed, cleared my throat, then yelled louder.

Not even a second later, Marco was by my side, running his hands along my body and checking me for injuries.

"I'm fine. Just got knocked down."

The sound of automatic gunfire got us moving. Back on my feet, I clutched a gun in both hands. The rest of our group fanned out after making sure we were all okay. I could hear the captains speaking with the bosses in the communication device Marco had fitted into my ear earlier.

I coughed again as we crept forward, making our way to the garage to exit out the side. As our group sounded off, we learned what areas were under heavy fire and went to assist. Marco was through the door first, shielding me from any attack. Men shouted as a barrage of gunfire rang too close to comfort.

There were guards everywhere, three times the usual number, working in an almost military cadence against the enemy. I caught a glimpse of Max and Stefano. Emiliana was in the fight, toe-to-toe against an adversary, gun firing, and knife slashing. Lil held two guns, as did Sofia. Marco's brothers, Trey, the doctor, and Nico, the accountant, were deep in the fray. Even Tony fought with us. I couldn't believe how much he'd changed.

I pushed that aside and took position with Marco as more Russians descended. We kept an eye out in case they were going to launch any more missiles. We fought. Time blurred as bodies fell. I felt the sting of a knife more than once as it made contact before I could dodge the impact. I blocked the pain as best as I could, numb to all but the next target, the next enemy that came at me or that I had to stop from double-teaming one of my friends.

Marco was a machine. I had to block him out as much as I could, or the way he moved and how he struck down our opponents would mesmerize me. I lost time as I fought. The night was a sea of bodies, a flash of weapons, grunts, and screams.

Then they pulled back. I couldn't believe it and glanced at Marco, who wore the same shocked expression but mixed with more anger. Our numbers were greater than theirs. Most of the corpses scattered across the lawn were theirs. Stefano barked out a few orders to the men, resulting in another flurry of motion as they hoisted bodies over their shoulders.

There was a large storage shed in the backyard, and as our soldiers carried the dead Bratva in that direction, I could only guess there were vats of acid or an industrial-sized freezer to stash them in until we dropped them on the Bratva's doorstep.

Marco was in front of me, his hand under my chin, tilting my head so that our gazes met and held. His gaze frantically bounced over my features then my body, cataloging the visible injuries. "How bad?"

"I'm fine. They're surface wounds."

He gave me a clipped nod then drew me into his arms. I

clung to him, so grateful that he was safe. I hadn't realized how much that mattered to me until we were faced with an explosion and war on our front lawn.

The bosses got to work, and Marco released me with reluctance, issuing orders to the men. I sought my friends, finding Emiliana covered in blood but grinning. Lil and Sofia were untouched except for a few splatters. We met halfway, all of us falling into one another for a group hug. I didn't care about the blood and neither did they. At that moment, I felt our connection solidify. We were a team, just as we'd always been.

"Come on. I'm sure some wine—or vodka—survived the shoot-out." I led them inside, and we moved around the kitchen until we located the hard liquor and shot glasses, all deciding we needed something stronger.

I downed two shots before a laugh bubbled up. After the third one, the glass tipped over as I set it down with an unsteady hand, my body shaking with mirth. "I don't think they'll come back tonight. That was—"

"Fantastic?" Emiliana grinned, sharing in the high of the battle with me.

I hadn't remembered her being so bloodthirsty, but I imagined being taken by human traffickers would change one's perspective on a few things. I mean, we were in the Mafia and already groomed for violence, but she'd been up close and personal in a way I didn't even want to imagine.

Lil looked around with a soft whistle. "What's the plan? Your house is trashed."

I shrugged, uncomfortable in my own skin. I was buzzing inside, and the vodka wasn't helping to quell it. *Where the hell is Marco?* I wanted him with me, immediately. "I'm sure we'll get it sorted before we leave for the lakefront place downtown."

Sofia settled on a barstool next to Lil. "You throw the best parties."

I grinned as I filled a shot glass then slid it in front of her.

"God, I missed you all. I didn't even realize how much."

"It must have been boring as a regular person without us around. How did that go for you?" Sofia downed her vodka, the question remaining in her amber eyes.

"I wouldn't say I adjusted fully." Laughing, I filled them in on my breaking-and-entering gig with Danny. "I did it as a favor to him but also to keep my skills sharp."

"Did he know who you were?" Em's skepticism was loud and clear. "Because the Bratva found you somehow. Could he have leaked the information?"

"I can't see Danny doing that. And I'm sure Marco already had him vetted. I'll ask." Eventually. Or not. I had other plans for him that night. I shifted, the heat in my stomach spreading. I was happy to hang out with my friends and immensely grateful that they'd arrived when they had, but I wanted everyone to clear out.

The guys flooded the space, and my gaze found and locked on Marco. The buzzing that had started from the adrenaline of the battle was a full-on body vibration at that point. I let him see everything I was feeling. I felt drunk, but it wasn't the alcohol. I hadn't had that much.

He came to me, settled his arms around my waist, and drew me against him. The possessiveness of his touch made it worse. *How much longer can I last? Seriously, why is everyone still here?*

"That was a little slow on their part." Trey threw himself onto a chair, pulling the vodka to him before pouring three fingers into a glass. He handed it off to his brother Nico. "Didn't you kill one of theirs in New Jersey? The wedding was the perfect place to stage their attack, but it wasn't until now?"

"Their hit man was midtext when I killed him. He jumped the gun and started to call in the kill after he shot El in the leg. We sent it along as if he'd finished the job then dumped him in the nearest garbage bin. I imagine he wasn't found right away, and not having identification on him didn't speed the process."

"Ah, it makes sense, then." Trey and Nico clinked glasses then downed their alcohol. "And I'm out of here. Early morning rotation at the hospital."

"Same, but not there." Nico smirked.

Nico was our banker. He handled our investments and ran the bank where we had our billions of dollars. Then there was the money laundering, which he also took care of, funneling what needed cleaning through our legitimate businesses. I couldn't get over the changes in him. He was so much bigger and broad like Marco, and there was a glint of ruthlessness in his eyes that I hadn't remembered being there before.

Stefano stood, taking Emiliana by the hand and pulling her to her feet before tucking her in to his side. "We're out too. You staying downtown?"

"Yeah. Thanks for coming to help out."

"Always." Stefano grinned, but it was dark.

I'd been wary of him when I was younger. There was something haunted and very dangerous about him. But Em loved him, and I wasn't going to pass any judgments. Besides, from what I'd learned, he was our capo, which meant he was everyone's boss, even Marco's.

Em pulled away from Stefano to hug me. "I'm glad we were here and that you're okay."

Sofia and Lil got up and hugged me. Then Sof launched herself at Marco. Their family was the tightest out of all five. When she drew back, she blinked tears from her eyes then gave us a jaunty smile. "I'll put a call in to my remodeling contact and pass your info along. Try to stay out of trouble!"

Marco and I said our goodbyes until the two of us were finally alone. I turned to him with one question on my mind before I shut everything else out but us. "Did you talk to Tom? Is everything handled that needs to be for tonight?"

"Yes." He nodded. "Our lives are short, El. Nothing is guaranteed. I'm done wasting time."

His eyes were hooded as he approached me with predatory grace. I met him halfway, launching myself into his arms. With a growl, he lifted me, his large hands on my ass until I wrapped my legs around him. He turned, and my back crashed against the wall, then his mouth was on me, traveling along my neck with open-mouth kisses before he scraped his teeth against my pulse point. A wicked thrill raced through me, and I tugged on his hair, desperate to kiss him. I tore at his shirt, and buttons flew in all directions, bouncing off the floor as they hit the wood. His mouth left my neck and crashed over my lips in a fiery collision that had my fingers digging into his shoulders.

We fought to get closer, clothes an annoying barrier. I unwound one of my legs so I could put my foot on the wall and push. Caught off guard, Marco took a step back, and I used it to my advantage. Dropping down to my feet, I shoved him back another few inches then struggled with the button on his pants. He yanked his shirt off then grabbed mine from the collar and tore it from neck to waist. Laughter spilled from my lips. I was drunk with lust.

We wrestled with each other's clothes until there were none left. He moved to the wall briefly then slammed his fist on a switch that caused a cover to close over the sliding glass doors, shielding us. Our soldiers would take care of the mess out there and patrol the grounds.

"There's no bed," he growled as he stalked back to me. Then he lifted me into his embrace with one hand supporting my weight under my thigh and the other buried in my hair, cradling my head.

"I don't need one." My voice was breathy and desperate, telegraphing how much I needed him. "I need you. Hurry." I knew his comment about the bed was partly a question to make sure I wanted this. But I'd already told him in the hot tub not to stop the next time, and I'd meant it.

We were on the move, his lips sealed to mine. Everything

faded. I didn't care about the destruction of the house or that we should leave sooner rather than later. I couldn't touch enough of him, and it was making me seriously mad. There was a crash as Marco swept the glasses and the empty vodka bottle on the island to the ground. Then he laid me on top of it, bared before him and so turned on I thought I would spontaneously combust with the slightest touch.

He climbed onto the island with me, but I wound my leg around him, pushing his shoulder with my hand, then flipped him. I wanted to be on top. I straddled him, rubbing against his length. A shiver traveled over my body as he gripped the back of my head then pulled my mouth to his. As his lips slanted over mine, our tongues danced together, tasting and teasing. The battle for supremacy continued, and my desire ramped up another impossibly high notch.

I braced myself against his wide shoulders, feeling the muscles bunch and flex as he moved. Then he flipped me onto my back, our mouths still locked together. He covered me with his weight. I felt him at the apex of my thighs, begging entry. I wrapped my legs around his hips and urged him to enter, breaking our kiss to meet his heated gaze.

He was at my entrance a tease of a second before pushing inside. My head knocked back onto the marble countertop, and he slipped a hand beneath to cradle it. When he was in all the way, he held still, and I gasped at the fullness.

I needed more and tilted my hips until he began to move slowly at first then faster. I met him thrust for thrust, my nails embedded in his back. My stomach clenched, and heat pooled in my lower abdomen. My body was strung tightly—I was so close. When his hand dipped between us, brushing over my small bundle of nerves, I fell over the edge, light bursting behind my eyelids. Another two thrusts, and he chased my orgasm with his.

His weight settled over me, and it felt so right. Then he was pulling out, and I whimpered at the loss. When he rolled to his back, he took me with him so that I was sprawled across him. He rubbed up and down my back, and I lay my cheek on his chest.

"I wanted to take my time with you for our first time." His voice was rough with desire, and I shivered at how the sound affected me.

"We can do that later. This was what I needed." I rested my palm over his heart. "I wouldn't have changed a thing."

"All I need is you, El." He kissed the top of my head then flexed his abs and sat up, pulling me with him before getting off the island.

He cradled me in his arms as he went to where our clothes lay scattered across the kitchen floor, thankfully not where the broken glass was. We dressed in what we could salvage. His shirt hung open because I'd ripped it off him, and there weren't any buttons. I put my panties, cargo pants, and bra on, but there wasn't a shirt I could wear. If our clothes had survived the explosion, they would be smoky and unwearable, not to mention wet from the fire system's sprinklers going off where they were still intact in that wing of the house.

I couldn't think about the damage. I loved the house already, but it was just a possession. Sofia said she would make some calls then pass the ball to me. The renovation would go quickly, and I knew we would be back before long.

Marco handed me a coat from the front closet, and I hastily put it on before we grabbed our weapons and headed to the garage. He let Tom know what we were doing, and a group of men went ahead of us to secure the area around our place in Chicago.

When his hand found mine, threading our fingers together on our way to one of the cars, everything settled in me. It was the two of us against whatever fight came our way. I couldn't have asked for anything more.

CHAPTER SEVENTEEN

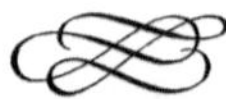

ELENA

I t didn't take long for us to arrive at the greystone building that housed our lakefront home in Chicago. I had clothes there, too, thanks to Sofia shopping for me and stocking both places. My biggest worry over the devastation of our house was that my wedding gown was in the closet. I hoped it survived. Mama had taken pictures that morning, but it would break my heart if the dress had been destroyed.

The night before, once Marco and I arrived at our top-floor living space, we'd showered together, and he'd delivered on his promise to take things slow. What started under the rainfall showerhead moved to our bed, where he worshiped every inch of me. My toes curled at the thought of everything he'd done and how deliciously sore my body was this morning.

I glanced at the time on my phone only to drop it back onto the bedside table with a groan. It was midmorning. We'd managed a few hours of sleep before his phone rang again and again until he gave up and got out of bed. I could smell coffee, and it lured me from my prone state on the comfortable mattress.

On my way to the bathroom to get ready before heading for

some necessary caffeine, I paused to appreciate the sight from our bedroom. I would never tire of the view of Lake Michigan from the wall-to-wall sliding-glass doors. I wished it was warmer because I would have loved to sit out there with my coffee. I would talk to Marco about getting year-round outdoor heaters on the balcony so we could do that.

It didn't take me long to brush my teeth and hair and get dressed. I followed the smell of coffee with my eyes half closed. Marco winked then set a mug in front of me as I slid my exhausted body onto one of the barstools. I inhaled the rich aroma before bringing it to my lips for that first satisfying sip.

I half listened and drank while mesmerized by the rolling waves outside the wall of windows, which were reflective so no one could see in. Lost in my thoughts, it wasn't until I heard Marco mention Yuri Pavlov that I pushed the fog from my mind and paid attention to what he was saying.

I caught bits and pieces but enough to know that he had new information. When he hung up and put his phone on the island, I pounced. "What did you find out?"

"The Bratva isn't where we originally thought they would be. They're holed up in an estate in Barrington. We'd assumed they would be somewhere downtown, which is what they've done in the past."

"But we have an address?" *Interesting.*

Intense green eyes met mine. "We do."

"What about a plan?" I needed to know the next steps because I was forming a plan of my own. There could be no overlap.

"We will soon. Today should be relatively quiet, and I have Tom here with another dozen men. Will you be all right if I take care of a few business issues?"

I wrapped my hands around the warm mug but waited to take another drink. "Like what?" If he meant anything with the Bratva, I was certainly not okay with staying behind.

"I'm going to the homes of our men who didn't survive the night to offer condolences to their families."

"I'll be fine. Do what you need to." Those families would be taken care of for the rest of their lives, and he was right. That couldn't wait.

"The girls will be over in about an hour. Enzo, Max, and Stefano will be nearby."

Perfect. I needed to run my plan by my friends. "That sounds good." I hopped off the seat then went to the fridge to grab the eggs. "Do you want some breakfast?"

Marco wrapped his arms around my waist from behind and rested his chin on the top of my head. "I would rather take you back to bed, but I'll take breakfast if that's all you're offering."

"Don't tempt me." I squeezed his forearm then pulled out the eggs, my mind still whirling with possibilities. His phone rang again, and I wanted to hold his arms around me so he wouldn't go. But he had to, so I gave in when he loosened his grasp around my waist, and I got to work on our breakfast.

The morning went by too quickly, and before I knew it, Marco was out the door, and the girls were entering loudly. They sported the same half-moons under their eyes that I did. It looked like their attack after-party had gone the same direction as mine. I couldn't help the grin that stretched my mouth wide at that thought.

With her finger, Emiliana made a circular motion in the air around my face. "None of that. We need coffee, lots of it, then some wine."

I was going to tease them, but I got her point. Sleep deprived wasn't a good state to be in. Coffee it was, then. I made more then set them up with mugs and creamer. There was a moment of silence while everyone took their first sip. When my gaze landed on Sofia, my stomach tightened painfully. Her cup was halfway to her mouth, and she paused with it suspended when she noticed my expression. "What's wrong?"

"The wedding dress you gave me. I don't know if it's destroyed or not, but even if by some miracle it's intact, there will be smoke damage."

Sofia covered my hand with hers and squeezed. "It's just a dress. I can make you another one if we can't get the smoke out or it's ruined."

I was having a hard time shaking it. It wasn't just the dress. Sofia had risked so much for me, putting her life on the line to save mine. The rest of the girls were silent as I struggled with the dress situation.

"I know what you're thinking." Sofia's voice was quiet but thick with emotion. "And I haven't done anything that you wouldn't have risked for me or any one of us. It's not about the dress, is it?"

I shook my head. "The arranged marriage between Enzo and me kept the two of you apart for so long when it should have never been there in the first place. And then you put your life in danger to help me, paying for it when Ivan tortured you. And"— I looked at each of them in turn—"I missed you all so much. Not only that, but I feel like I betrayed you by leaving. And worse, I brought the Russians to your doorstep when I returned."

"Forced to return," Sofia said, and I snorted in response.

So true.

Lil came around the island and wrapped her slender arms around me. "That's crazy. We all would have wanted you safe, and if any one of us had been approached by Katya to help you, we would have."

Emiliana and Sofia joined Lil in a group hug with me in the middle. I fought the tears misting my eyes then gave in as a few fell. Even though I hadn't been born into royalty like they had, it was another one of those moments when I knew without question that I was one of them. It helped me put any past insecurity behind me and silence the little girl who had always known she was different.

"We've got your back. Always," Emiliana reiterated. "When Marissa died, the three of us vowed to be there for each other, no matter what. That includes you, El."

The floodgates opened with that. By the time I got myself under control, we were all an emotional mess. Lil broke out the wine, and we settled on the couches in the living room. I had to talk to them about what I wanted to do and see if they were on board.

"Did any of you hear where Yuri is staying in Barrington?" I knew of the suburb. It was a surprise. I would have thought he'd be in Chicago.

"I did," Emiliana said as she tucked a long strand of dark hair behind her ear. "I have the address. Why?"

"Great." She was married to the capo. I should have expected her to be the one who knew. "I need it."

"What are you doing, El?" Lil leaned forward, her elbows resting on her knees and silvery-blond hair framing her face.

"I'm in, and"—Sofia held up a finger for us to wait while she downed half her wine in one gulp—"I don't even care what it is."

I grinned. "I want to break into the house the Pavlov Bratva is staying in and have a little one-on-one chat with Yuri."

In a slow side-to-side, Emiliana shook her head then leaned back against the couch. "I didn't expect that, but count me in."

Lil rolled her eyes. "As if any of us wouldn't be. But I don't see how you can sneak inside with all their soldiers there."

"We need blueprints if we can get them and an accurate count of soldiers patrolling the grounds, at the very least." I sank my teeth into my lower lip, worrying it while I thought. "It's going to be hard to do this without the guys knowing. I'm not sure how we'll put that off."

"Easy." Sofia clapped her hands, her eyes sparkling with mischief. "They have a meeting soon where all the bosses will congregate. I think that's happening—"

"Tonight," El interjected. "I'll make sure I'm working out in our super-secure gym. Stefano won't worry about me. Lil, you can get the plans?"

"I should be able to. We'll have to slip our guards and meet at The Coffee Stop."

Part of me felt bad about deceiving the guys. "I'm not sure about sneaking behind their backs, but there's no way they would let us go. Or me, anyway, since I'm the only one who will go inside."

"Ah, I never agreed to that." Sofia crossed her legs then downed the rest of her wine before setting it on the table. "Why would it only be you going in?"

Because I wouldn't risk them, and it was bad enough they were involved at all. "This is what I used to do for my friend from college. Remember I told you about Danny and his security business in New Jersey? Wait"—I couldn't believe I hadn't thought of it before—"he can get the plans for us. I'll give him a call." He owed me. I hadn't accepted money from him when I did all those jobs because I didn't need it. Sofia had made sure I had more than I would ever need when she got me out. "Sofia, can you pick up the things I need for the break-in? I can give you a list." She nodded, and my mind continued to whirl, given how quickly we were moving.

"If you'll have the specs, why are we on the outside?" Emiliana asked.

"I need you guys to act as lookouts from around the property. It'll be easier that way, and we can communicate through the earpieces. I still have mine from last night."

Sofia pursed her lips but agreed. Then Emiliana and Lil did as well.

I laughed. It had to happen. I looked forward to the confrontation with Yuri. We needed to end whatever was going down with them, and I wouldn't risk the Bratva hurting my friends to get to me. The countdown until I had answers was underway.

CHAPTER EIGHTEEN

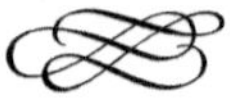

MARCO

The elevator opened with a swoosh, and I stepped out, searching for El, needing her more than I would admit. The day haunted me. The tactile grief I'd witnessed from the families of our fallen men was still fresh in my mind. They had known the risks, but that didn't change the deep sense of loss, the devastation of losing a loved one. The unpredictability of death was a part of life, though, however hard it was to accept when it hit home.

I locked on to El as she set a dish filled with pasta on the island before she came to me. When she was within arm's reach, I pulled her into my embrace and dropped my head to the crook of her shoulder, inhaling her scent. Her skin was so soft and inviting, and I wanted to stay there for the rest of the night—*if only I could.*

She squeezed me tightly, and we remained unmoving, existing in a moment of shared grief. I pressed a kiss to the fluttering pulse at the base of her neck then drew back, wanting to hear how things had gone for her, desperately needing a distraction. "How was your time with Emiliana, Lil, and Sofia?"

She grinned. "It was a lot of fun. I'm glad they came over. How did everything go?"

I caressed her cheek, enjoying how she shivered in the wake of my touch. With her, I wanted more—always more. But it wasn't the time. I guided her toward the couch, needing a few minutes with just the two of us so I could share what she seemed to want to hear. The pasta could wait.

I tugged her with me as I dropped to the couch. "It was rough. Tom went to some of the homes, and I took the families of the men I had the most interaction with. We were lucky the number of losses wasn't higher. The worst hit was from that damn rocket launcher. A fucking delivery truck." I shook my head in disbelief. "That was a new one." We'd never seen them coming. It was a smart move and not one we'd expected from the Bratva.

El snuggled against my side, her gaze focused on the dancing flames in the fireplace she must have turned on earlier. "Sofia's contact reached out to me, and I got them started on the renovation. We'll have to go over the plans, but they're clearing things out already."

"Good. I'll have a few men oversee them." I grabbed my phone and sent a text to Tom, asking him to get that underway.

"Are you hungry? I made food."

I forced a smile. "I thought I smelled something. And yeah, I could eat." As I stood, I pulled her to her feet. "I hate to do this, but I have another meeting tonight. I won't be gone too long."

"That's fine." She shrugged then went to the kitchen, averting her face.

That's weird. Why isn't she making eye contact? "Is everything okay? Are you sure you're not upset about me leaving again?"

"Yeah, it's fine." She waved off my concern, still not looking in my direction as she busied herself with the pasta and dishes. "I didn't do anything elaborate. I thought about making carbonara or lasagna, but then I didn't." She set the plates on the island.

I grabbed the wine she'd taken out, uncorked it, and poured each of us a glass. We sat at the island for a casual meal. I wasn't up for the dining room table, and it seemed she wasn't either. We ate in silence for a few minutes, each digesting the day we'd had and what was coming. Maybe I was imagining things, but my gut nagged that there was something she wasn't telling me.

Elena

When we finished eating, we rinsed the dishes and put them in the dishwasher. Marco refilled our wine, and I tugged him back to the living room. Before we sat down, I peeled off his suit coat and laid it over the back of the couch. I wished he would take his shirt off so I could trace his sexy-as-hell tattoos with my tongue. But we didn't have the time. "When do you have to leave?"

He glanced at his Rolex before answering. "In about half an hour. Thanks for making food. I didn't realize how hungry I was."

"No problem." I studied him for a moment, visually devouring his striking features. He was so attractive. If he wasn't a badass Mafia boss, I swore he could have been a model with that incredible bone structure and body that promised hours of satisfaction. I could wash clothes on those abs. And none of that was surprising, as his mom had been a supermodel. But beneath the hotter-than-sin good looks, something dark lurked—in his eyes, a storm brewed.

My phone pinged from an incoming text, and I casually glanced at Sofia's question about having picked everything up I'd asked for.

Emiliana: *I'm good to go—commencing workout bait and switch.*

Lil: **thumbs-up emoji* All good here.*

Me: *got the blueprints!*

I bit my lip. Guild washed over me about involving them. *What if something goes wrong? Or the guys find out? They would be so angry. And Marco... would he forgive me?*

Me: *you guys can back out if you want, no hard feelings.*

They all messaged with middle finger emojis. I guessed we were on. I fought the smile curving my face and tried to look innocent as I tucked my feet under me and swiveled to face Marco. My knees pressed against his thigh. "Is there something else that happened today?"

He faced me, his gaze a little too inquisitive, and I worked harder on pushing all thoughts about tonight from my mind.

Another second passed before he responded to my question. "Yuri and I spoke. It was a heated discussion, and the main point of it was that he won't stop. He demands your life for the loss of his son's."

"We know that already." I had a hard time understanding why he seemed like this call was any different from the other with Yuri.

"We do." Marco threaded his fingers with mine before he pulled me onto his lap so that my legs straddled his and we were face-to-face. "I won't let that happen. You're my wife, and it's well within my rights to end him if he tries to harm you."

I pressed our foreheads together, longing to feel his lips on mine. "I've survived him this long. He won't get to me." When he drew me closer and took my lips in a toe-curling kiss, I melted against him. My mouth opened, and he deepened the kiss, his hunger clear in the masterful way he dominated. When I moaned, he swallowed the sound.

The way he kissed wove a spell around me, and I knew there could never be anyone else. There was no more denying how I felt. He was everything I'd dreamed. I'd had a crush on the boy, but I loved the man. I needed him more than my next breath.

When he pulled back, we were both breathing heavily. His intense green irises were eclipsed by the desire in his dilated pupils. I wanted to tell him that I loved him, but the fact that I was going to lie to him tonight made it an inopportune time.

He lifted me off him and deposited me on the seat next to him. "I have to leave for the meeting, even though I would much rather play with you."

I grinned, because yeah, I would have liked that too.

"Are you sure you're okay with me going out? I have extra security around the building, and we have people watching Yuri too. There's no way he'll get another opportunity to strike us while we're unaware again."

A thrill shot through me at what I would be doing soon, and Marco narrowed his eyes. *Oh no, is he on to me?*

CHAPTER NINETEEN

ELENA

I waited ten minutes to make sure Marco was gone, on his way to meet with the other bosses. There was no way to get a car out, but I could sneak past our security. Before I left, I opened the email from Danny. He'd delivered, as I knew he would. The specs on the house the Bratva were staying in, along with a live satellite feed, hit my inbox just as the elevators closed behind Marco. I studied them and plotted the best entry point. There were multiple cameras that I would have to steer clear of, but several blind spots would let me hide between guard rotations.

I changed into my go-to deadly pants that Sofia had given me when I made my escape all those years ago. It was a good thing they had been among the few spare clothing items in my backpack when I made a run for it and that I'd left them at the condo instead of taking them with me to the suburban house. Some tools I would need later were also in the slim pickpocket kit I liked to use.

A thin, fitted black Henley was the next item I considered necessary for stealth missions. I had a stocking cap and gloves with me, but my hair was black, and the moon was barely a sliver outside. The darkness would provide enough cover.

I couldn't waltz out of there without our guards alerting Marco or our captain stopping me. I went to the elevator that granted access to our main living space and dropped to the floor. With my fingers and the help of a steel nail file I had specifically for that purpose, I manually pried apart the doors. When they were wide enough, I positioned my back against one side and used a foot to hold the doors open. Next, I put on thick gloves to protect my hands and held a penlight between my lips before grabbing the strong metal cable.

Ready, I let go of the doors and was plunged into darkness, aside from my minuscule light, but it was enough for me to see. As quickly as I could, I used a combination of maneuvers to slide and climb down until I reached the top of the elevator car. Opening the door on the ceiling, I lowered myself until there was only a minimal drop then shoved the gloves into a side pocket in my pants—I might need them later.

It was the tricky part, and the guilt of deceiving Tom, our captain, and most of all, Marco, had me hesitating for a moment too long.

I tracked security and located blind spots as naturally as I breathed, so I knew what to expect with our guards, their patterns and rotations.

I checked my watch. I could make it between our guards' rotations, but it would be tight. Better to wait until the next soldier was past the point where I waited to exit in that sweet spot that allowed five seconds before another guard began his rounds. The window was narrow. Marco and Tom knew what they were doing.

But I was one person, not an army, and very good at what I did.

There was a reason Marco had nicknamed me Little Thief. I was going back to the roots of what my birth mother and Mama helped mold me into, once again assuming the guise of a thief in the night.

When the second hand on my watch reached the all clear time, I flattened myself on the floor of the elevator car to work the doors open with my fingers at the bottom and in between the metal.

When it was barely large enough for me to slip through, I did. Pressed against the wall, I moved to the grill for the air shaft entrance not far from the elevator, which would take me out of the building without detection. Crouched down and in the shadows, I used my nail file to unscrew the panel. When it was open, I slipped inside, making sure to put the panel back in place to cover my path. I paused long enough in the ventilation system to text Lil that I was in and to pick me up in five. I made quick work of winding through the small space until I found myself at the outside vent.

The screws were rusted, and I had to lean in for added torque, struggling to loosen them. A black SUV passed, and I cursed under my breath at missing Lil the first time, my hands sweating in the effort to hurry. It took a little longer to get the screws undone. By the time I did, I was a full two minutes late.

As soon as I climbed out and onto the city sidewalk, I covered my tracks, making sure everything was in place once more, then rushed to the SUV across the street that was driving by at a moderate pace. When Lil saw me, she slowed enough for me to wrench open the back door and throw myself in.

"I can't believe you got out." She turned to me as I climbed into the front seat, a wide grin on her face.

A black stocking cap hid her light-catching blond hair, and she wore clothes similar to mine.

"I'm sure it was equally difficult for you."

"Nope. We played that old game of I'm at Emiliana's, Sof said she was at my house, and… well, you get the idea."

I laughed. It was too easy. "If only that would have worked

for me. I'm surprised it did for Sofia, since she's on Yuri's hit list too."

Lil turned the corner and headed to The Coffee Stop, which was Mafia owned and where we'd planned on meeting before heading to the Bratva's location. She parked in the alleyway behind the coffee shop, which was closed for the night. We got out of the SUV and went through the unlocked back door. Lil drove home the bolt once we were inside. Soft lighting led our way through the back hallway, and the incredible smell of roasted coffee beans lured us farther. It was addictive and made me long for a caramel latte.

The thin light beneath one of the doors was the only indication of where Sofia and Emiliana were. Lil moved in front of me and said, "They're in the break room."

Lil opened the door with a flourish and swept inside. "We made it!"

Emiliana stood closest to us and tapped the face of her watch with a fingernail. "It's about time."

Sofia snickered from her comfortable position on the couch. There was a shopping bag by her feet, and I made a beeline toward it. Before I could wrap my fingers around the handles, she yanked it to her chest and held it hostage. "Not so fast. We have some plans to see first."

Emiliana fell into a chair, waving her finger back and forth. "You're not keeping us in the dark. That isn't how this is gonna go down."

I rolled my eyes and took a seat next to Sofia on the blue cushions. "I hadn't planned on shutting you guys out. Danny forwarded me the specs just as Marco left our place." With a few taps on my phone's screen, I had the blueprints pulled up. I'd already highlighted the problematic areas and mapped my entry and exit points. I took a screenshot and sent the image to their phones then set mine on the table so we could all look at it.

I explained the route I would take and why. After answering

a few questions, I showed them the safest places I'd located for them to observe the grounds and report back to me if there were any changes in what we expected to take place.

"So did Danny wonder where you are?" Lil plopped down on one of the chairs across from us.

"No. I told him in the beginning that there would be a chance that I would disappear and if I wasn't able to contact him, he shouldn't attempt to find me." He was a good friend, and it was a little tricky to pull away as I had, but it was necessary. "He asked if I was okay, but he respected what I'd told him." When the war with the Bratva was over, I would talk to Marco about visiting him someday. He was a brilliant guy, close to genius level, and could be an asset.

I would have felt bad involving him in my life, but he worked with dangerous people from time to time. It was probable that we could help him in the future, too, should the need arrive.

Sofia snapped her fingers near my face. "Come back to us. The window is quickly closing before the guys figure out what we've done."

"Hey." A wave of regret hit me hard at her statement. "You guys don't have to do this. The last thing I want to do is cause problems for you all."

Emiliana rolled her eyes. "We're a team. This is what we do. Now, shut it, and let's roll."

I laughed loudly. I loved them. They were family. It had only taken me almost a decade to realize how much they meant to me and that I wasn't as different as I'd thought. I was accepted even without royal blood flowing through my veins. Marrying Marco had given me power, but they didn't care. I was still one of them, no matter what, and I would never take it for granted again.

"I'm driving." Sofia jumped to her feet, releasing the bag of gear I'd requested as she headed toward the door.

We piled into a black SUV similar to what Lil had driven earlier. I got into the back with Lil. Emiliana rode shotgun, and Sofia took the wheel. As we flew through the streets then onto the highway, I riffled through the bag of equipment. The black sports harness needed to go on first. After pulling it out of the bag, I secured the leg loops and waist belt then added the D-shaped carabiners to attach the flipline. There were slings to secure my shoes that I would need for the inside job and the spikes for climbing. The rappelling gear was in there, too, and I got to work, prepping what I would need. I secured my guns in the shoulder harness and shoved my hands into the gloves.

I checked the feed Danny had hacked into to verify that Yuri was in residence. When I got confirmation, I breathed a sigh of relief.

Sofia dropped Lil off first then Emiliana. Finally, it was Sofia's and my turn. We parked down the way, out of reach of the streetlamps. When I got out of the car, careful to close the door quietly, I moved around to make sure there were no clinking noises. I was missing one piece of gear. Before I could ask, Sofia had opened the trunk, reached inside, and handed me the grappling hook pistol.

Through the inky darkness, we sprinted toward the designated spot that would be safest for Sofia. The air was crisp with the promise of rain, which only spurred me to increase my pace. Our window was closing. Once Sofia was hidden near the last house closest to the sprawling manor the Bratva was hiding in, I changed direction to the route that would most quickly align me with the large oak on the property's west side, where the master bedroom was and my point of entry. If there was one room that didn't have cameras in it, my guess was that one.

I skidded to a stop and crouched behind a mound of bushes. It was a good thing the grounds were heavily landscaped. I double-checked the timing of the soldiers as they patrolled to the information Emiliana and Danny had reported. A slight shuffling sounded as the grass flattened beneath a heavy boot. Pungent cigarette smoke teased my nose. I held my breath as the guard came within feet of my hiding place. He paused as if sensing something was amiss. I didn't dare move a muscle. In my right ear, I listened as Lil, Emiliana, and Sofia gave whispered accounts of what they saw. Sofia's harsh whisper for radio silence once she spotted the guard near me cut off all chatter.

Another five seconds passed before he moved away. I held still, waiting until Sofia gave me the all clear. I was only partially visible to her, but even that was beneficial. I had only seconds to toe off my shoes and hook them to my equipment before I shoved my feet into the spikes. The flipline, attached to my left hip, looped around the trunk and secured to another ring on the opposite side of my belt. I made quick work of scaling the tree, not stopping until I was far above the next soldier's head. Sweat beaded along my hairline at the hurried pace. I held still when he came within hearing distance, not daring to give away my position with even a slight scraping noise.

Unlike the other guard, this one didn't pause. As soon as there wasn't a risk of him hearing me, I shimmied up another few feet so that I was above the roofline. I maneuvered onto a branch with my back to the trunk. I was far enough from the roof that jumping was too risky but was in the right proximity to shoot the pistol. There would be a noise, and I would have to wait before rappelling.

I was in place then whispered through our communication link that I needed a distraction in two minutes. Lil responded that she called it in. We were close to the fire station, and she'd contacted someone we had in our pocket. I kept an eye on the rotation below and my watch. The second hand ticked agonizingly slowly, but I had to hold out for the planned commotion or the guards that surrounded the house would hear me.

When it was almost time, I took aim. Right away, the sound of sirens followed by blaring horns screamed through the quiet night as a fire truck barreled down the main road not far from where we were. My finger squeezed the trigger, releasing the grappling hook and wire. I secured one end to the tree then attached my rappelling hook to the line and pushed off, flying toward the roof. The small amount of noise I made was muffled by the fire truck's racket. My feet touched the roof, and I adjusted my position to maintain my balance.

My footing secure, I switched out the connections so that I could rappel down the side of the house to dangle in front of the designated bedroom window. With sure feet and precision, I moved to toe the edge of the roof then pushed off. It didn't take long until I was where I needed to be. I removed the glass cutter from the bag on the back of my waistband and got to work. In no time, I freed the lock, opened the window, and got inside.

The room was dark. Based on the time, I didn't expect anyone to be there, but it would have been helpful to find Yuri right off the bat. I whispered to the girls that I was in then tiptoed through the room, stopping at the door that led to the hallway. There was an office downstairs and two sets of stairs. The back one was closer. There was no way I would make it to Yuri without encountering a few guards.

Light filtered into the hallway from a few open doors and from the first floor, where I guessed most of the Bratva soldiers to be. I crept along the wall on silent feet. Voices carried, and I wished I knew what Yuri sounded like. I'd seen a picture of him, though—I wasn't flying entirely by the seat of my pants.

In one hand, I had a tight grip on my gun, silencer attached. In the other, I palmed a knife. The first open door was inches from me. I waited, listening. A woman stood alone to the side, her back to me, angry words in Russian pouring from her mouth. As quickly as I could, I passed the gaping doorway. The other lit rooms didn't contain people, and I crept down the back stairway, my gun leading the way. Male voices exploded around a corner, and I backstepped out of sight. When they faded, I hurried down the remaining stairs, my heart thudding as I came closer to being discovered by the Bratva.

Two doors stood between me and the office. When the one closest to me opened, I flattened myself against the wall, hoping the poorly lit hallway would help to disguise my location. But the man turned, surprise etched on his face as he went for his gun. I moved quickly, slamming the butt of my Glock into the side of his head before he could pull his weapon out. As he dropped, I tried to grab him and take as much weight as possible to muffle the noise of his fall.

I peeked into the room he'd exited, a bathroom—lucky. My nerves were strung tight, and I tasted bile, frantically swallowing to keep it down. Hooking my arms under his shoulders, I dragged him into the room, pressed the button on the knob to lock the door, then shut it quietly behind me. I sprinted to the room I thought was the office, unwilling to take any more risks by moving slowly. It was a small miracle I'd only encountered one soldier.

The office door was ajar, and I squeezed inside, ready to shoot anyone who wasn't Yuri or his son, Vic. I blinked to adjust to the brightness of the room then firmed my hand, shifting my aim with a line on the man who'd stood from his desk at my entrance. Light-blue eyes met mine, and I quickly scanned his blond goatee with a smattering of gray, cropped hair, and a barrel chest.

I'd found Yuri.

CHAPTER TWENTY

MARCO

"It's decided, then." A deep sense of satisfaction coursed through me at the near conclusion of the meeting with the bosses of the Five Families—my friends. "We attack at midnight, pending Stefano ensuring Camila is safe, ending Yuri's reign once and for all."

Stefano slammed his fist on the table. "Agreed."

Enzo and Max gave their consent, and a rush of satisfaction flooded me. El would be safe. A few more hours, and we would strike our enemy from the board. I glanced around the warehouse where we held such meetings. It was close to the lakefront but secure enough that we didn't worry about drawing too much attention. There were no windows on the ground floor, and the name on the outside made it clear that it was a building for boat storage. The calls that came in about renting space were told it was full and redirected to a sister site we had in place to keep suspicion away. Not that it mattered. We owned Chicago.

I turned to Stefano. "That'll set Vic up to run the family." He had to have been relieved, as it would give his sister another layer of security with Yuri gone.

"That would be ideal." Stefano pulled his phone from his pocket and clenched his jaw.

I knew he was reaching out to Camila. We wouldn't go ahead with the ambush unless we were sure she was safe and not at the mansion Yuri and his army were occupying. We had one more thing to address before we left to go home to our wives.

It was difficult to leave El for the handful of hours I'd been gone during the day and again for this meeting. I'd increased the guard, and we had intel on the Pavlov house. There'd been no movement reported, but that would change. We had to strike before they recouped to come after us again.

A loud scrape sounded as Max pushed back from the table, about to stand. I had to stop him. We had to discuss the last topic. "Any news on Lil's half brother?"

"Yes. We know where Luc is," Max said, his mouth in a grim line. "There's no point in going over details of his life yet. We'll figure out how and when to bring him into the fold after ensuring El's safety. We have time."

If he was handling running two families, his and Lil's, I wouldn't press the issue. I rapped my knuckles on the table then pushed to my feet as Enzo swore.

"We have a problem." He lifted eyes crazed with a blend of fear and rage. "Sofia is five hundred feet from the Bratva's location."

Stefano launched to his feet, his body radiating anger as he checked his phone. "So is Emiliana."

Ice infused my veins, and I cursed myself for not adding a tracking app to El's phone. We were together all the time, and it hadn't seemed necessary.

El's cagey response when I told her I had to step away for the meeting suddenly made sense, as it seemed she had plans of her own. "Let's go get them." One question had to have gone through their minds, as it did mine—*is this when we'll wage war against the Bratva, rather than in a few hours?*

My hands shook as I texted El for her whereabouts. We tore out of the warehouse, piling into our separate vehicles. Stefano took the lead then Enzo, Max, and I jostled for position, but I edged them out. We careened through city streets, blowing lights with no fear of the police stopping us as we headed for the highway.

Through my Bluetooth, I connected to Tom. When he answered, I could barely contain my fury. *How the hell had she snuck out?* "Check for El. I have word she may not be in the building."

Tom swore then issued orders to my men to search the area while he checked the top floor where we lived. A handful of minutes later, his voice came through the line. "She's not there. We're going over the other floors and garage. Let me call you back."

I hit the disconnect button then pushed my foot harder on the pedal. Images of what could happen to her flashed through my mind in horrific and vivid detail. My hands gripped the wheel so tightly that I wasn't sure I would be able to peel them off when I crashed through the front of the goddamned mansion.

Everything was a blur outside the windows. Spotlights over the exit signs and brake lights pierced my skull, threatening a massive tension headache. I needed the destination for what the guys saw on their maps or I was going to go crazy. *Five hundred miles from his house where? Were they in the back, on their knees execution style? Were they dead and laid out already?* I couldn't reason, and when my phone rang through the speakers, I grabbed hold like a lifeline and pressed the button to answer.

We took an exit as Tom's voice came through my Bluetooth connection. "We found two vents that had been unscrewed. One by the elevator in the garage. The other on the street. She must have used them. I didn't see any signs of struggle, and there was no suspicious activity, no one that would have caused alarm."

"She's with Sofia and the others. Be ready in case I need you." I didn't tell him why or where. He didn't need that. Tom would react and come prepared to wherever I told him if the time came for that.

I disconnected then called Enzo. "Where the fuck are they?"

"Same place. West side of the property. I'm taking us straight to them."

"Not in the mansion or the backyard?"

"No." Enzo clipped the word.

I disconnected. We weren't far. I had a gun in the console next to me and two in the holster. I was ready to do whatever needed to be done to get El out of there and to safety.

Once off the highway, we flew through suburban streets. It was late, and there weren't many cars on the road, as it was a weeknight. Enzo swerved, narrowly missing a compact car. They managed to slam on their brakes as he blew through a red light. The rest of us followed in what had to have appeared to be a high-speed chase.

A few more near misses, and we were a thousand feet from our destination. My mind tunneled to one thing only: get to El. Enzo took the next two turns, and we passed sprawling mansions with professional landscaping and few streetlamps. It wasn't until the last turn that I caught sight of the small cluster of women near a tree and an SUV parked at the curb. The closer we came, so did a black Maserati.

CHAPTER TWENTY-ONE

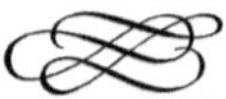

ELENA

Yuri towered over his desk, unmoving. He was a brute of a man in his late fifties but in the physical shape—at least from what I could tell from a glance—of his early forties. With a soft click, I shut the door while keeping my gun trained on him. I took measured steps away until I was in front of the Pavlov boss. My communications link was open so the girls could hear what was going on.

Neither of us said a word, taking in details about one another, assessing. There was something vaguely familiar about him, but I chalked that up to pictures I had seen. Thankfully, I hadn't had the displeasure of meeting his eldest, Ivan. *Was Yuri a psychopath like his son? Was his youngest, Vic?* I needed to know what I was encountering. None of the intel indicated Yuri or Vic were psychopaths like Ivan had been, and I hoped that was true.

Guttural Russian words spilled from his mouth. I understood a majority, but it was hurried, and I didn't know if Lil, Emiliana, or Sofia spoke the language. "English," I snapped.

"Goddamned. She did it," Emiliana whispered in my

earpiece. I tuned her out, needing to focus all my concentration on Yuri.

He paused then switched to English. "In the pictures, you had brown eyes."

"Contacts." I raised an eyebrow because that was an odd thing to say, given that I held a gun on him. "I'm here to negotiate. Your life for a cease-fire. What do you say?"

His gaze flicked to my gun then back to my face and my hair, only to return. "What is the natural color of your hair?"

Weird. Does he think he was going after the wrong person? "Enough. This is how it's going to happen. If you don't agree to call off your attacks and leave the Families alone, I'll kill you. It's your life or a cease-fire."

"Your—"

The door opened, and a man walked in, speaking Russian and addressing Yuri. I knew him instantly. Victor—or Vic, as he preferred to be called—Yuri's youngest and only remaining son was a carbon copy of his father, but with darker eyes. Ivan had been the one with the same pale-blue orbs as his father.

He whirled and started to raise his gun when I yelled, "Stop! I'll shoot him before you take aim."

"Oh shit." Vic's head knocked back, and his lips parted as if there was more he wanted to say, but he just shoved his gun back into the shoulder holster. Yuri cleared his throat, breaking the wide-eyed trance Vic seemed caught in before he turned toward the sound. Father and son hurtled Russian words back and forth at a speed I struggled to follow, so I didn't bother. They seemed to agree, and Vic's tense shoulders relaxed somewhat before he turned to me, his hand extended. "I won't hurt you, but you need to get the hell out of here. Now."

Yuri said nothing. Instead, he watched me with narrowed eyes, his face leached of color. He had barely moved a muscle since I entered the room.

I firmed my stance. Even though my legs were already

locked at shoulder width apart, I wasn't sure I could move, given the tension of the situation. "I'm not going anywhere until Yuri and I have an agreement or he's bleeding out on the floor."

A wide smile split the older man's face. It was the strangest negotiation I'd ever had. It was my first, but still, it was crazy weird. "I need an answer."

"You don't want to do this, Elena." Vic edged closer, and I tightened my already firm grip on the Glock. "Put the gun down. I'll get you out safely."

I could have laughed, because *really*? But Vic was married to Stefano's sister, Camila, and because of that and how they interacted, I believed Vic.

A curt nod was my answer from Yuri. It wasn't good enough. I held firm, wanting to glare at Vic as he inched closer but refusing to take my eyes off the man in front of me. "I need the words."

"I will not kill you, Elena." His voice was rough and held some emotion I couldn't quite place. "The attacks will stop."

"We must go." Vic's hand rested on my bicep, and he gently lowered my gun. I didn't take my eyes off Yuri as Vic inched me toward the door.

I yanked my arm away once we were clear. The hairs on the back of my neck stood on end. I wanted out of there in a bad way. Nothing good would come of getting caught, deal or not. Yuri could go back on it and have me killed.

"What the hell were you thinking?" Vic whisper-shouted as he moved around me and grabbed my arm again. "You're complicating things. I had it handled."

We paused at a closed door, and after opening it, he yanked me into a bedroom. I wrenched free. A woman whirled around, her eyes going wide, and I stopped in my tracks. "Camila?"

I hadn't seen her in years, not since her father, Frank Rossi, married her to the enemy to absolve himself of his part in my mother's infiltration of the Pavlov empire. Her dark-blond hair fell to her shoulders with a few long bangs framing her heart-shaped face. But what made me pause was her lack of fear, aside from the surprise of seeing Vic drag me into their room.

"El," Camila said with a sigh. "You shouldn't have come."

"Who is that?" Emiliana screeched in my earpiece.

"Camila, my God, it's been so long. I had no idea you were here. Does Stefano know?"

"No"—Emiliana whispered—"he's going to be so pissed that I didn't get word to him."

My hair covered my earpiece, so no one knew I had ears on the conversation. But I agreed with them about one thing: I had to get out of there.

"Ah, we have a problem," Sofia chimed in. "The guys are on to us and headed this way—damn tracker app. I thought I'd disabled it."

"This isn't a 'we' issue—you guys leave. I can get out on my own." My words were for the girls, but they worked equally well for Vic and Camila. They had no idea I was talking to someone else.

Vic's gaze dropped to my harness and the rappelling equipment attached to the front. "That's not an option. If word gets out that you're here, thanks to your confrontation with Yuri—and it will—it'll be impossible to escape the way you planned."

Anger infused me at the implication that his father would go against his word. I took a step toward the door, which Vic blocked. I should have killed Yuri when I had the chance. But there was still time…

My gaze narrowed on Vic, analyzing the best way to get around him. He stood as if on the balls of his feet, leaning toward me, his expression pained yet oddly hopeful.

"Stop, Elena. There are things you don't know. Camila and I will get you out, but we have to get to the garage without anyone spotting you."

"Why would you help me?" He was an ally of sorts, but this

was strange. Time was moving too quickly, and my body tensed, waiting for the alarm I knew should be sounding. The pounding of feet as soldiers swarmed the room. The inevitable pop of gunshots.

"I'm not the enemy here, but we need to hurry. I'll explain more when we're away from here."

"Wait." Camila moved between us. "If El goes out the window from our bathroom, she'll be close to the garage. If you redirect the guards around that corner, she can slip inside if we take the Range Rover parked at the end."

"I don't see why you need to give me a ride. I can make it across the grounds without being detected." They were making it more complicated, and I didn't want to be in the car with them. That would make it too easy to kill me then dump my body. And while I should trust Camila, she could have flipped sides. She was living among the Bratva and had been for a number of years. My fingers twitched then tightened around my gun. "No. This isn't a good idea. I'll leave on my own." Besides, I needed to reconvene with my group, I hoped before Marco arrived and a bloodbath ensued.

Vic must have seen the stubborn set to my jaw because he held up both hands, palms out. "El, please. There are things we need to talk about, and this gives me the opportunity I wouldn't have had before. Just give me five minutes in the car while I get you far enough away from here. You'll have your gun, and there isn't anything to worry about from Camila and me."

I weighted my options, how long it would take me to reach my friends and defuse the situation once Marco inevitably arrived, as opposed to driving to them. Then there was the way Vic and Camila reacted around each other, which calmed my fears a bit. Their expressions softened when they looked at each other—it was glaringly clear that they were in love. I clenched my teeth until my jaw ached, finally coming to a decision.

Their obvious affection for one another and the eagerness of

Vic's reaction to me added a layer of comfort that they weren't going to kill me... unless I was wrong, and they were going to shoot me in the car. I tilted my head, taking in the tension of Vic's posture and how he lifted his hand as if to squeeze mine but dropped it back to his side as if thinking better of the physical contact. I gave myself an internal shake. My instincts had never been wrong before, so I nodded and agreed to their plan.

"Give us a few minutes to get to the garage and tell the guards they're needed inside on Yuri's orders. That'll get them moving."

"Five?" I checked my watch.

"Yes." He pointed to a door off the bedroom. "Bathroom is that way." Then with Camila's hand in his, he hit the lights. I heard the sound of the door opening, saw a brief flash of light as they exited the bedroom to the hallway, and registered the click of it shutting.

That was my cue, and I went into the bathroom, located the window, and opened it. Rather than kicking the screen out, I pulled it inside then set my hook and tested to make sure it was secure and would hold me.

I cupped my hand around my watch to hide it before depressing the small button that lit up the screen so I could keep track of time. When there was only one minute remaining, I positioned body in the window frame then lowered myself outside so that my legs leveraged against the outer wall and my gloved hands had a solid grip on the rappelling rope. Those few seconds between patrols were all I needed, and I pushed off, falling fast, only slowing by squeezing the rope when the ground neared.

I crouched behind the bushes then sprinted for the corner, knowing that the next guard would see the dangling rope and sound the alarm. I peeked around the edge of the house, noted the lack of guards in the vicinity, and dashed into the dark with my heart slamming against my rib cage.

A SUV's door opened. I recognized Vic and lowered my gun. Camila was already sitting in the passenger seat. I dove into the back seat, and Vic shut the door then got in, started the engine, and backed up. I lay across the floor to hide.

"Stay down." The vehicle slowed, and I guessed we were exiting the driveway to the street, where more soldiers would be stationed. I couldn't wait any longer, and I made contact with Lil, Sofia, and Emiliana through my watch. "I'm headed out. Can you guys get to the car? I'll meet you. Hold on." I popped up cautiously to speak to Vic. "Where are you going to drop me?"

"At your car or Stefano's place, which I would prefer."

I caught the way Vic took Camila's hand in his. Maybe my little expedition was the perfect excuse for Camila to see her brother.

"Emiliana, can you stop the guys, and we'll meet you all at your house?"

"Are you on the phone?" Vic met my gaze in the rearview mirror as I sat on the seat rather than the floor.

"Yeah, in a way." I grinned. *Does he think I broke in and confronted the Pavlov boss without any backup?* His furious expression made me pause. "Drop me at the next block. I have a car waiting there."

"Emiliana," I prodded, needing to know my little expedition hadn't caused the guys to go into full-on war mode.

"We have a problem," Sofia responded instead. "They're already here."

CHAPTER TWENTY-TWO

MARCO

The Maserati squealed to a stop. The door opened as I punched the button to lower my window so I could shoot out the side. A woman flung herself out, hopped onto the car, and slid over the top, her long blond hair trailing her agile movements. When she landed on her feet, she launched herself at Emiliana.

Enzo hit his breaks. Smoke curled from the tires as he skidded to a stop. The rest of us did the same as a glint of light from our headlights shone on the blade that was at Emiliana's throat. She—because it was clearly a woman, even though I couldn't see her face—extended her arm and pointed a gun at Sofia's temple. Lil was off to the side, her mouth hanging open. It'd happened too fast.

With guns out, we were in front of our cars, all four bosses, ready to lay down our lives for the women we loved. It wasn't until we were closer her face. I searched the area in a frantic attempt to find El. *Where is she?*

Lights flashed then another car screeched to a halt. Doors opened and closed, but I couldn't move a muscle.

"What the fuck?" Enzo growled.

I recognized the woman holding weapons on my sister and Emiliana. It was Katya, the goddamned Pavlov Bratva's angel of death.

Rage surged through me, followed by an injection of adrenaline at the sight of Emilana at knifepoint and my sister with a gun aimed at her temple. I wanted to end Katya. Every fiber of my being demanded the satisfaction of putting a bullet between her eyes.

All around us, it was pitch black. We were in a standoff, congregated near the tree. Headlights from our vehicles were the only source of light. In the distance, the mansion where the Bratva was in temporary residence loomed. Soon, they would notice the cars and come to investigate.

Headlights bounced in my peripheral vision as tires screeched to a halt. I registered the doors opening and closing but couldn't take my eyes off the gun directed at my sister.

"True colors, Katya?" Enzo growled.

"What's the point here, Kat?" Sofia asked, casually looking at her nails.

Katya's lips twitched. My sister amused her. I sucked air slowly through my nose, taking everything in. Emiliana didn't look alarmed either. The threat wasn't what it appeared to be. "Where's El?"

"Right here."

I whirled around. She stood next to a black Range Rover with Vic Pavlov and Camila. She flinched when she caught my gaze then glanced to where the rest of the girls were. "Well, this is unexpected."

"Don't shoot Vic." Katya's calm, accented voice sliced through the night.

"As if they would. You can stop playing now, Kat." Sofia winked as she stepped forward, only to be pulled roughly into Enzo's arms.

"Stand down, Katya." Vic moved to Emiliana's side, blocking Katya from a direct shot when she lowered her gun.

Emiliana went to Stefano, who looked like an artery would burst from restraining himself from harming the assassin.

El sank her teeth into her lower lip as she stood before me. "I'm sorry, Marco. I had to confront Yuri, and I knew you wouldn't have been okay with it."

Her words slashed into me with the same agonizing effect as a dull blade. I grunted in acknowledgment, unsure what to make of her actions. We would deal with whatever she thought she should do without confiding in me later. All I cared about was that she hadn't been harmed. Closing the distance, I pulled her to my side, needing to feel that she was warm, alive.

"We need to leave. There isn't much time. Seconds, really." Vic motioned for us to get in our vehicles. "Camila would like time with you." He indicated Stefano with a nod. "We could all meet you at the house in Chicago, on the lake."

Stefano grunted a response, his arm secure around Emiliana's waist. The rest of us said nothing, but we would be there.

Lights bounced in the distance, and I reacted by grabbing El and pushing her toward the passenger seat in our car. The Bratva was aware something was amiss and would soon be in pursuit. If they didn't know it was us and that we were close, we stood more than a chance to get out of there undetected.

El buckled in as I got the car turned around then floored it toward the highway. I took a different route than the others. It would be better to add confusion if we split up until we reached the expressway could hit top speeds.

"Marco—"

"Don't. Not right now, El." I tried to gentle my tone, but the climbing harness she had on spiked my anger again. I didn't want to yell at her, though. The fact that she was alive and next to me was all I would focus on for now. "We'll talk when we're home. Without an audience."

Elena

I pushed my toes into the floor as Marco flew down suburban roads, the sign for the highway within sight. There was so much I wanted to say, but he was mad, and rightly so. I should have talked to him about what I wanted to do. Maybe he would have worked with me. The possibility of him not agreeing was what had spurred me into action. But conferring with Danny... *what will he think?*

My stomach was a mass of knots, and I felt sick at the thought that I'd betrayed his trust. He'd done nothing but tried to help me. "I'm sorry. I should have talked to you about what I wanted to do."

"You should have," he snapped.

His tone triggered my defenses, and I wanted to shout at him, to snap my comments right back. But that wouldn't have solved anything, and he had a right to be upset. I'd put my life in danger and potentially given the Russians something they could use as a bargaining chip against him—myself.

I needed him to understand why it was easier for me to do things myself, that going to him felt foreign when the decision was mine. "I've been on my own for a while now, and I've gotten used to doing what I think is best, not answering to anyone. It's difficult to change my thought pattern, and it feels a little like I'm giving up my freedom."

"That's the thing, though, El. We're partners, equals in this relationship. I'm furious because you put yourself in unnecessary danger and because you didn't trust me enough to talk to me about what you wanted to do."

"I do trust you." My heart was breaking. While I didn't think what I'd done was entirely the wrong thing, he had a point about talking things through and trusting each other.

"El, we're not going to resolve this right now. We're almost at Stefano's. Let's shelve this conversation until we're home."

I pursed my lips to keep from saying anything more. Silence filled the space between us. I caught sight of Enzo and Sofia in the car next to us, and it looked like they were arguing. *This is a shit show.*

We got off the exit that would take us to Emiliana's. It didn't take long before we all pulled into the private underground parking for the building they owned. After Marco parked, I got out but waited for him. Once we were all there and crammed into the elevator, I touched the back of Marco's hand with mine. When he turned his over and threaded our fingers together, the tension in my chest eased slightly. We would be okay. I wasn't foolish enough to think everything was fine, but it would be after we hashed out a few things.

Once inside, Emiliana took out a couple of bottles of wine and vodka. I was in the mood for booze, needing the numbness it would deliver much more quickly than wine would—especially since we drank that all the time and were pretty immune to it.

By the time everyone had something to drink and was either seated or standing around the island, the central gathering place in all our homes, it seemed, I realized we were missing someone.

"Where's Katya?"

"My father called her back to take care of the equipment you left behind." Vic's jaw pulsed as he delivered that little tidbit of information.

"Why would he do that?" It didn't make sense.

"My guess is because he finally realized what I've known for years." Brown eyes met mine with an emotion I couldn't quite place. "For the first time, my father saw you up close and was able to recognize features that you share with Daniela. You're my sister, Elena."

CHAPTER TWENTY-THREE

ELENA

Halfway to my mouth, the shot glass slipped from my numb fingers, clipped the edge of the island, and violently crashed to the floor, shattering into tiny pieces, just like my world. *"You're my sister."*

Everyone stared at me. It was hard to breathe. I felt Marco's arm sliding around my waist, and I leaned against him. *It's not true.* I scanned Vic's face, looking for any similarity to mine. I didn't see a single thing about us that looked alike. So I said the only thing I could to his ridiculous statement and rejected his claim with a simple "no."

But it was out there, and I saw by the conviction in his eyes that he wouldn't take it back. My knees turned to rubber, and Marco's arm tightened. *Why is everything spinning? And is it darker in here?*

We were moving. Marco's arms were tight around me, and he cradled me to his chest. For a brief moment, I felt safe, sheltered. I wanted to close my eyes and block everyone out except for Marco.

But it was there, in the back of my mind—the *possibility* that I had Russian blood flowing through my veins—*royalty*, but not the kind I wanted.

From far away, I heard voices murmuring as if I was under-water. One was my lifeline, and I clung to the deep baritone. I let my eyelids drift shut and focused on breathing, as Marco instructed. I blocked the other sounds, not ready to face what-ever it was that waited for me. I felt it, though, an ominous pres-ence that would change everything.

"Back the fuck up."

Marco snapping at our friends penetrated, and I pushed the darkness away as guilt swam through me. *I can do this*. The last thing I wanted was to appear weak. I wasn't. I was a freaking force to be reckoned with, and that was the image I had to portray to Vic—*who is my not-brother*.

Several blinks, and the world came back into focus. A few more, and everything sharpened to normal. Marco's arms were like steel bands around me, and from my angle, his jaw looked like granite. I knew that if I faced him, I would see the ruthless, determined expression he wore to take on an army.

My heart skipped a beat, and I reached up and cupped the side of his face. When he tilted his head down so that our gazes met, I telegraphed through my eyes how much he meant to me. My body softened, and tears misted. He was my rock. I needed him, and he never hesitated, even though I might have the blood of our enemy running through me.

We were on the couch. He'd tried to give me some privacy, but everyone had followed and grouped around us. It was time to deal with the bomb Vic had dropped.

"I'm all right." My voice was thready. I cleared my throat and banished my fear. "Just needed a minute."

Arguing exploded around us. Sofia, Lil, and Emiliana were yelling at Vic. Stefano had to wrap his arms around Emiliana—the fists she was making made it clear she was close to attack-ing. The tears I'd been keeping at bay slipped down my cheeks in twin rivers. Their actions said more than words—I was still one of them.

When I pushed against Marco's chest, he released me but remained nearby, our thighs touching. I met Vic's gaze. "I don't believe you."

He reached inside his suit coat, and everyone pulled their guns out. Marco was on his feet in an instant, his large body blocking me from view. I swiped at the tears, deeply touched by how they came to my defense. I leaned around Marco to see what Vic had been going for. My not-brother stood with his hands up and a dark scowl marring his face.

"What the hell do you think I was going to do?" Vic growled between clenched teeth. "Shoot my sister?"

"Yeah." Sofia rolled her eyes. "It's what the Bratva has been attempting since she was little. And Ivan. Let's not forget what your brother wanted to do to her."

"I'm not Ivan." Vic lost some of the anger, but the disgust remained in the downturn of his lips. "There's an envelope in the inside pocket of my jacket. That's what I was reaching for."

Marco stepped forward, yanked the side of Vic's suit open, then withdrew a white envelope. Slowly, everyone lowered their guns but kept them in hand. My gut churned at whatever new information we would learn. *Is it a note from my mother?* I couldn't imagine what Vic had on me.

When Marco reclaimed his place next to me on the couch, I glared at Vic, unable to look away. Vic shielded Camila behind him, but she moved back with an annoyed expression directed at Stefano, her brother.

"I've known for years." Vic's voice gentled. "I had an idea that you could be my sister and had Katya watch over you on occasion, but I needed to know for sure. When I heard my brother had been dispatched to find and kill you, I'd sent Katya to help hide you and, in the process, obtain samples of your DNA."

"When she staged my death." I remembered the day well.

She'd cut me and used the blood to soak my shirt in specific places, adding tears from the knife that would have inflicted fatal wounds had the shirt been on me at the time. In addition, she'd taken a few strands of my hair. Everything had gone into a bag, and she'd flown to Italy and planted the evidence in one of the human trafficking sites before strategically bombing it, making sure that my clothes survived well enough for my family to find.

"The blood that coated the knife and a single strand of hair was held back and used for the test."

"And Yuri?" His name tasted wrong, rolling off my tongue. "Did he know?"

"Not until tonight, when he saw you in person for the first time."

"Then how did you have an accurate test done?"

Marco had opened the envelope and unfolded the paper. He swore under his breath, but I refused to look. I would face it after I had my answers from Not-Brother.

"Katya was able to get a sample when she bandaged an injury. The hair was easy, taken off a comb from his bathroom."

There was no more stalling, as I didn't have additional questions. Marco had the papers between us so that we could both read them. I glanced down, and bile climbed my throat as the undeniable truth was in black and white before me. Yuri was my father, and Vic, my half brother.

I sucked in a breath, my hand spasming by my side.

Marco dropped the papers and clutched my trembling hand in his. With two fingers underneath my chin, he turned me toward him. "This changes nothing. It's a complication, nothing more."

His meaning was clear, and I gasped at the truth of what he said as it resonated through my entire body and soul. He loved me. I was his wife. Nothing else mattered. And he was mine. I would fight for him until my last breath.

Vic's phone rang, and he pulled it from his pocket and raised it to his ear as he answered in Russian. He moved away, and Camila went to Stefano and drew him to the side to talk.

Stefano enveloped Camila in his arms, and I was glad they were able to have that moment. *How long had it been since he laid eyes on his sister?* Too long was my guess, possibly since the day his father, Frank Rossi, sent her to marry the enemy.

Not even two minutes later, Vic came to me and reached to hand me his phone. "It's Yuri. He wants to talk to you."

Marco intercepted and took the phone. I was fine with that. *What am I going to say? Do I even want a relationship with the man, my father, who has been trying to kill me all my life? It isn't a hard decision. I don't.* There were questions, but as far as building a connection… I couldn't see that working.

"No."

I tilted my head, wondering what Marco had responded to. "She'll contact you when she's ready. Otherwise, stay the hell away from her."

Marco disconnected the call and tossed the phone back to Vic. Then he addressed all of us. "Yuri called off the manhunt for El."

I sagged in relief. Yuri was keeping his word, and thanks to Marco, I could live in denial until I was ready to deal with my father—if I ever was.

CHAPTER TWENTY-FOUR

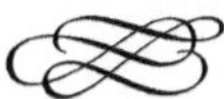

ELENA

I was never so glad to be home as I was when we stepped off the elevator of our lakefront greystone home and into the inviting living room, the soothing backdrop of the water visible through the floor-to-ceiling windows. I glanced at the kitchen, weighing what to do. I'd only had the one shot of vodka before my world imploded, but for some reason, I didn't want anything else.

Marco had glued me to his side since I arrived with Vic and Camila, and he'd continued to touch me in some way—our thighs on the couch, his arm around my waist if we were standing around, his fingers woven with mine if we were walking. It was the most reassuring sensation, something I hadn't realized I needed. If I'd known how amazing marrying and falling in love with that man would be, I never would have run from my family. I would have stayed to fight, knowing they could handle whatever complication landed at our doorstep. But I was younger then, and the what-if game wasn't always the best one to play. I needed to focus on what we had in the present instead of looking into the past and wondering.

He released me then pointed to a blanket. "Bring that onto the patio. We're going to talk out there."

It had gotten even colder, as it was nearing midnight. "Why not in here?"

He grabbed tumblers and splashed two fingers of whiskey in each before his hooded gaze lifted to mine. "Because if we stay in here, we won't be talking, and there are things we need to discuss."

A jolt of desire slammed into me from the heat in his eyes and passion lacing his words. I wanted to get to the part where we weren't talking. Gathering the blanket in my arms, I went out onto the balcony with Marco on my heels.

After I got settled on one of the chairs, the fleece throw wrapped around me to ward off the chill, he handed me a tumbler. I had been wrong earlier. Another drink would ease the pending conversation.

There was no doubt about what we were going to talk about, and I took a tentative sip of the amber liquid before deciding to kick off the discussion by defusing things. "I can't say enough about how sorry I am for not confiding in you."

Marco downed his drink in one gulp then set the glass on the small table between us. "I know. And even if you had come to me, I'm under no illusions that you wouldn't have gone regardless of my thoughts on the matter."

I remained silent because he wasn't wrong.

"Our marriage is new, and compromise is going to be tricky until we master it. My main issue is your safety and you not trusting me enough to come to me with what you wanted. I may not have agreed, but I would have found a solution we would have been happy with."

"That goes both ways. I won't live by standards that you don't comply with."

Marco rubbed a hand across the back of his neck. "I can do

that in most circumstances, but there are decisions that are made on the spot and need immediate action."

I got it. He was the boss of the La Rosa family. I could understand that and make some allowances. "It's going to be a work in progress." And it was. "But I do trust you. And I will come to you when the next situation arises." Because there would be one, and I would do what I planned and include him out of respect and love in the process next time. He was a brilliant man with my best interests at heart. "Are you upset about my involving Sofia?"

He snorted. "My sister is a handful and Enzo's problem."

I laughed because if she'd heard that, she would have kicked him in the shin. God, I loved my friends. When I met his eyes next, the burning desire reflected in the almost-glowing green caused heat to pool low in my belly. We were at the next part of our evening—the one I wanted above all else. "We're done talking now?"

"I could have lost you," Marco growled, dark promise swirling in his eyes. He crowded me, and I wound my arms around his neck as he drew me close. The blanket fell in a puddle on the chair. "I need to touch you, taste you, imprint myself on you so that it's burned in my psyche that you're here and alive."

The things he did to me with words alone... heat licked over my skin in a warm flush as he lifted me, pushed the balcony door open, then walked us to our bedroom.

Broad shoulders flexed as he moved, and my pulse fluttered at the base of my neck. *So gorgeous.* My fingers twitched with the need to explore the well-defined contours of his body, tracing the taut skin etched with intricate tattoos over his biceps, one of his pecs, and along his arm.

When we got to the bedroom, he released my legs, and they slid down his hard body in agonizing degrees. Then his mouth was on mine, coaxing, demanding, drugging me. My senses spun at his sensual assault. I buried my fingers in his hair and tugged him closer, my lips plumping, bruising from the intensity. I wouldn't have had it any other way.

There was a moment of push-pull between us as we tore at each other's clothes, desperate for skin on skin, neither of us playing around. The near brush with death, with the possibility we could have lost the other completely, infused our desperation.

Our clothes lay scattered at our feet, and I launched myself back into his arms. My hands traced his wide, shoulders as the muscles shifted and bulged then ran down his back before he lifted me. Cold air hit my skin as he deposited me onto our bed. My mouth opened in shock, but my protest died on my lips as he dropped to his knees in front of me, yanking my body toward him then spreading my legs.

My desire surged in anticipation, and suddenly, his mouth was on me with such intensity that my back arched. He teased my clit with his tongue, delivering an onslaught of sensations in the wake of his masterful caresses. Electricity sizzled through my body with his every move. When he inserted a finger then another, sending a dizzying wave of desire through me, I gasped, my world spinning out of control.

In tandem with his tongue, he thrust in and out of my body while rubbing, sucking, and scraping his teeth over that sensitive bundle of nerves, and I quivered with need. When he curled his fingers deep inside and pushed against my clit, I exploded, hurtling over the edge. The world paused, suspending me in a hyperaware state of tantalizing euphoria. Vaguely, I was aware of him lifting me.

My legs automatically wrapped around his waist as my vision cleared enough before he pivoted, took a few steps, then pressed my back against the wall and his hard length at my entrance. He held one of my legs just under my thigh, while his other arm wound around my waist, my shoulder blades resting against the wall. Then he was pushing inside. Stars exploded, and I screamed as a second climax slammed into me.

His powerful thrusts continued, and then I was falling again, whimpering from the loss until my back hit the mattress and his heavy weight was on me but not in me, and I clawed him closer, needing more. I would never have enough of him.

When he pressed against my curves, a guttural moan rumbled from his chest. His corded muscles flexed and bulged under my fingertips as he trailed kisses along my neck. I tugged him back then met his passion-filled gaze, shifting languidly beneath him as he hovered near my entrance.

A seductive, crooked grin curved his lips as he slipped his hand between our bodies. When his fingers traced my seam, I cried out, arching higher to meet his touch. I needed him to fill me. Inch by inch, he entered, his expression intense, hungry, and filled with so much love that I whimpered.

With each thrust and dizzyingly hungry kiss, sensations built until I was gasping for air, a sense of urgency feeding my hypersensitive nerves until I exploded around him in quivering convulsions. He trailed open-mouthed kisses along my neck then whispered my name, heightening the aftershocks of my orgasm. Then his moan vibrated against my skin, and he chased my climax with his own.

He tugged my body against his. Enveloped in his embrace, I relaxed, tangling my legs with his as he pressed a lingering kiss to my lips. Minutes passed as our breathing evened out, and we lay together.

"I would do anything for you. I love you more than I could ever express, El." His words were rough.

My stomach flipped at the depth of emotion in his declaration. I tipped my head back, my cheek pillowed on his chest. "I know you would. I would go to hell and back for you too. I love you, Marco. I think I always have."

Nothing more needed to be said, and I sank into the security of his embrace. It wasn't long until we fell into an exhausted, contented slumber.

CHAPTER TWENTY-FIVE

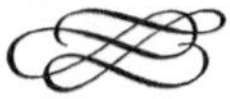

ELENA

I awoke alone in our big bed to the view of tumultuous waves and an overcast day. A light mist coated the glass doors leading to the balcony. The heavenly scent of coffee and bacon permeated the air, and I spread my hand over the indentation where Marco had slept. The sheets were cold. He'd been up for a while. After last night, I'd needed the extra sleep and was grateful he hadn't woken me.

With a flick of my wrist, I threw the covers back, shivering in the chilly air. I staggered to the bathroom and got ready. After a I showered, brushed my teeth, and dressed, I made a beeline to the kitchen for some desperately needed caffeine. Marco was at the island, a sexy-as-hell grin coming to his face as I neared. He handed me a steaming cup, and I planted a kiss on his talented lips.

"Morning." He tugged me close then repositioned me between his legs so my back rested against his chest. "I thought we could spend some time together before I check in with Tom and get a few things done."

I snuggled against him as he wrapped his arms around my

waist, then took the first sip of the day. *This is the way to wake up.* "I'd like that."

"How are you feeling since talking with Vic yesterday?"

A twinge of unease marred my happy state of mind. "I'm not thrilled about it. Who would be? I found out I'm half Russian and related to a Bratva boss. Not exactly my dream evening."

"It doesn't change anything, but it may explain how much vodka you drink."

I snorted. "If that was the only side effect, this wouldn't be an issue."

"There's no issue." He turned me in his arms, took my coffee, and set it on the island. "You're my wife, a La Rosa. Yuri has no claim on you."

I wrapped my arms around his waist and rested my cheek on his chest. His words resonated, but the situation continued to bother me. "When I was young, I felt different. Adopted by Nicole and tolerated by Antonio into one of the most powerful families, I didn't feel the Mafia princess title that Nicole claimed was mine. But as Yuri's daughter, I am one. Just from the wrong Mafia."

The soothing motion of his hand tracing circles on my back eased some of the tension after revealing part of what bothered me the most. He'd already eliminated the fear of rejection by claiming me throughout the night, whispering words of love and that nothing had changed. He told me over and over again that I was his and he was mine and that nothing else mattered. It meant more to me than I could ever express.

"You're my family," Marco reiterated. "The supposed ties to Yuri and Vic... that's just a connection. We can use it to broker peace."

"Isn't peace even more dangerous than war?" I teased.

Marco chuckled, and the warmth of his laugh infused my bones. "Always. But we'll work the angle. You can get to know them as much or as little as you want. I'll be by your side the entire way."

I pushed out a breath, releasing the last of the tension in my body from our discussion. It was time to put it to rest. I would talk with Yuri later that day but with Marco present. "It's crazy how we got to where we are. From childhood crushes to enemies to partners. You're the love of my life."

"I'm the lucky one." Marco tipped my head back with his fingers beneath my chin. Then his mouth was on mine, and the conversation was over.

As his lips expertly moved over mine, the familiar heat built inside me, and I molded my body to his. I could have kissed him for the rest of the morning.

When he pulled back, my body was happily buzzing and wanting so much more. But I knew there were things both of us had to do, and when he spoke next, he confirmed just that.

"I made you breakfast. Eat, and then I have to get some work done."

I climbed onto the stool while he uncovered the eggs and bacon he'd kept warm for me. "I want to call Nicole and let her know what happened last night in case Max hasn't filled her in."

"I'm sure she'll appreciate that. I'm going to run down and talk with Tom now. He's outside on the lakefront side waiting for me. Come down if you want." He pressed a kiss to my forehead before heading to the elevator.

I swallowed a mouthful of eggs then called after him that I would be down shortly. Five minutes later, after eating breakfast and putting the dishes into the dishwasher, I slipped on shoes and headed to the ground floor and outside to meet Marco. I'd grabbed a coat and my phone and wanted to walk along the beach to talk to Nicole, as the threat from Yuri was over.

When I stepped off the elevator into the underground garage, two of our soldiers fell into step behind me. Marco must have let them know I was coming. Oddly enough, it didn't bother me. Other than the time I'd spent in New Jersey, soldiers surrounding me had been a common occurrence. And I felt lighter, freer, after all the talks Marco and I'd had.

The cool breeze whipped through the exit from the building onto the sidewalk, and I zipped my coat all the way up. Marco stood not far away, his dark hair ruffled in the wind. An air of danger clung to him, and my pulse quickened. My stomach fluttered as a thousand butterflies took flight at how tall, imposing, and devastatingly handsome he was—and he was all mine. I grinned and waved, motioning with my phone in my hand that I was headed to the beach. He nodded, gave the guards trailing me a pointed look, and then went back to his conversation with our captain.

It was relatively early, but cars whizzed by on the one street I had to cross to get to the sand. I waited until the light changed and the busy morning commuters had to stop. With quick steps, I got across and sank into the sand as I headed toward the rolling waves that crashed along the shore. I would never tire of living close to the water. If it wasn't for the outdoor paradise we had in the suburban home, I wasn't sure I would want to move back there. As it was, I'd lived around some form of water for so many years that there was no way I would give it up.

I pressed Nicole's contact, brought the phone to my ear, then waited for her to answer as I strolled next to the breaking waves. Seagulls squawked overhead, and a mix of dark and light fluffy clouds crowded the sky. It would storm soon, based on the number of darker ones and the whitecaps dotting the lake.

"I was just thinking about you," Mama said.

I grinned, not surprised she'd said that. She always had that sixth sense if something was wrong. "I hope those thoughts were good."

"Darlin', you know you brighten my day. Now, what's going

on? My instincts are screaming at me that something happened."

Case in point… "Did you talk to Max yet?"

"No. Why? Should I have?" Her voice tightened a tiny bit with worry.

"I only asked because of what went down last night." I filled her in about the excursion the girls and I had planned, the guys busting us, the conversation with Vic, and Yuri calling off his attack. My fingers gripped the phone in the silence that ensued after I finished with that last part.

"I know what you're thinking, and this changes nothing. You're my daughter and have been since you were a little girl. Yuri is a sperm donor. That's it."

She had a unique way of looking at things, and I burst out laughing. It was good to get her perspective. "I agree, even though we don't know the whole story. Daniela took that with her to the grave."

"Mm-hm. Wonder why she did that?"

I did too. And I might never know, but I was oddly okay with that. "Not sure, but it all worked out. She met you, and having you in my life was the best thing I could have asked for."

"Aw, Baby Girl. You're my heart. You know that, right?"

"Always." And I did. I knew that no matter what happened she would be in my corner, unconditionally.

"You're not worried about how Marco feels, are you? Because that man has had a crush on you forever."

"He and I are good. But I'm going to talk to Yuri later today, just to get that out of the way. I don't want a relationship with him, and I would be surprised if he felt differently."

I heard my brother, Tony, in the background, and she murmured a distracted hello back to him. "You could be surprised. He might want to get to know you."

"Maybe. It doesn't matter, though. I'm not ready for anything more than knowing he's my biological father. I like my life the way it is with Marco. We're finally on common ground. I have you, and I don't need anyone else."

"I'm happy for you. Tony is motioning for the phone, so I'm going to hand you over. Come by soon. I miss you, Baby Girl."

"I will." I chatted with Tony for a few minutes, filling him in on everything I'd already told Mama. He'd changed so much. In the past, he wouldn't have given me a second thought. It seemed everyone was better without Antonio in our lives. My other line beeped, and I glanced at the caller ID but didn't recognize the number. When we hung up, the same number flashed across my screen again, and I took a chance and answered it.

"Elena?"

The deep, heavily accented Russian voice caused me to stop in my tracks, my toes curling into my shoes, digging the tips into the sand. *Why is he calling me?* "Who is this?"

"Yuri Pavlov."

"You're supposed to wait until I'm ready to talk to you." Chills danced along my body, and I shivered, burrowing deeper into my coat. I stood frozen, anticipating his response.

"I've never been very good at waiting, and… you need to know a few things. Your mother—I cared for her very much."

"Funny way of showing that. You did have her killed."

"It's more complicated than that."

I pivoted toward the lake, my gaze bouncing over the rolling waves. The chilly air blew my hair back from my face. I pinched my lips together, refusing to say more but also not ready to hang up. He had information about my mother, and I wanted to hear it.

"Your mother was so beautiful."

"And your wife isn't?" I'd seen pictures of Mischa's chilling beauty. The woman was stunning but terrifying.

"Mischa is indeed lovely, but she doesn't have the same allure as Daniela. There was warmth and effervesce about her.

She had such passion for life, and her laugh, it would fill the room, making everyone smile. I loved her."

"And again—"

"Elena, she disappeared. She was just… gone. When I found out about her betrayal, it was already too late."

I staggered back then caught myself. That was unexpected. Needing to move, I resumed walking along the shore. "Are you saying you didn't have her killed?"

"No, I did not. But I'm not saying I wouldn't have when I learned of who she was and why she was there." He didn't speak for a few seconds, his truth hanging in the air between us. "That's not the only thing I wanted to talk to you about. I realize that you've made your choice and you're with the Italians, but I want a relationship with you, even if it's only a phone call twice a year."

"Why, because I remind you of my mother? You don't know me at all. I don't understand the purpose."

"Please give it some thought and call me when you're ready."

I shook my head. "Fine. Goodbye." I hung up then pivoted to go back to the house when I heard a muffled thump as if something heavy had hit the sand not far from where I stood. My hand automatically went to my gun. Then I saw her, a classic, willowy beauty, standing between my murdered guards.

A loud pop cut through the gusting noise of wind and waves before I could take aim and squeeze the trigger. Two prongs latched on to my legs, and jolts of electricity shot through my body, causing every muscle to tense as I dropped to the ground.

CHAPTER TWENTY-SIX

MARCO

I checked the time while Tom and I discussed how he would implement the new security plan after I talked it over with El. My gaze crawled over the expanse of beach, stopping on a random food shack or public restroom here or there. Something wasn't right. She should have been back by then. "Have the guards with El checked in yet?"

Tom furrowed his thick black eyebrows. "No. I'll radio them."

I sent her a text then headed for the street as Tom radioed her guards. I jogged across, my 9mm pointing at oncoming traffic to stress how they'd better stop and let me pass. I wouldn't let another second go by without making sure with my own eyes that El was safe. My gut churned. A part of me already knew that something was wrong.

I sprinted to the beach, my feet sinking into the loose sand. Digging in with the toes of my shoes, I pushed harder in the direction she'd gone. Seagulls took flight, scattering out of my way as I raced through a flock of them.

Off in the distance, midway up the beach, two bodies were slumped over. They were too large to have been El, but their bodies could have blocked hers from view. It took me a few minutes to reach them. *Goddammit!* Both her guards were dead. I scanned the area nearby for any clues that would tell me what had happened.

They took her.

I could hear the pounding of shoes not far behind me and didn't bother to look over my shoulder. Tom would have sent several men after me.

I studied the terrain. A gun lay in the sand near the dead guards—El's gun. The angle was strange, as was the imprint in the sand. The main thing I took away from the evidence was the lack of blood. *Please be alive.*

I will get her back.

My men fanned around me. Tom issued orders to have the deceased removed. While they were lifted and carted off in the direction of my home over two men's shoulders, I called Vic.

Tom left to check the security feed while half the guard stayed behind with me. The loud drum of my heart superseded the roar of the waves as the weather picked up. The wind whipped loose granules of sand to pelt us, stinging my skin where they struck. I turned so that my back was to the gusts and the spray of mist from the crashing waves.

Vic answered on the second ring, and I barely let him finish his greeting before I growled. "Where the fuck is El?"

"What do you mean?" His deep voice rose in alarm. "She was with you last night. That's the last time I saw her."

"Twenty-five minutes ago, she went for a walk on the beach. Her guards are dead, and she's missing without her gun. Find out if your father took her."

I hung up without waiting for a response then called Max. As soon as he answered, I repeated what had happened. "I need all hands on deck to find her. We were lured into a false sense of security."

"That was a smart move on Yuri's part. Do you think the documents were faked?"

"I don't know what to believe at this point. They could have been." I hung up, knowing he would call Stefano and Enzo, and ran back to my building, needing to see if Tom found anything on the security feed.

Fucking hell! I didn't even want to think about how brilliant their plan had been or how stupid I was for falling for it. I should have done my own test before buying in to anything handed to us by the Russians. The clincher was that Vic was supposed to be on our side because of his connection through Camila to Stefano, our goddamned capo.

I slammed through the door to the security room on the first floor of my building. One thing was certain: I would kill anyone in my way of getting El back.

———

Elena

My head throbbed, and my neck muscles screamed at me. I took stock of where I was as I surfaced from unconsciousness. As much as I could, I tried not to give a sign that I was awake as I strained my ears for any sign of another person nearby. I couldn't move. My legs and arms tingled because of the awkward way I was restrained to a hard chair. My body ached. Ropes bound my waist, and my hands were secured behind my back. My head hung forward at an uncomfortable angle.

The slow drip of blood from my temple must have been caused by Yuri's wife hitting me with the butt of her gun. She was a hell of a lot stronger than she looked.

"You're awake."

Dammit. There was no use pretending anymore, so I lifted

my head, my sore neck muscles screaming in protest. Even with the Russian accent, her voice was like a fine whiskey. I could see the appeal.

It was the eyes that got to me—indifferent, calculating. I got the impression that even though she wanted me dead, it wasn't raging jealousy or anything like that. She was too cold, and I hoped she wasn't like the stories I'd heard of her eldest son, who my friends had told me was a psychopath.

The room I was in was rather plain. Rain splattered against grimy old windows and hammered the steel roof and walls. We were in an office inside a warehouse. The only furniture other than the chair that held me was an old gray metal desk shoved against a wall to one side. "Why am I here?"

Her long fingers trailed over the desk. I didn't want to look too closely at the items in the unrolled black bag that sat atop it.

"I could have shot you, especially as you're so difficult to kill. But that would have been too easy. My son's death is your fault." She pursed her lips, the only outward sign of emotion. "Instead, I decided I would get to know you in a way that would give me some satisfaction. Your death will be an atonement to him, a gift."

So she was the one behind the last attempt? I notched my chin higher, fighting for a bravado I didn't quite feel. "You'll be dead soon."

Her face remained impassive. "Is that any way to speak to your stepmother?"

Yeah, no. "You're nothing to me."

"We should get acquainted, then." She opened the door, leaned out, then yelled in Russian. A few seconds later, two burly men came in. One had a cart with a device I was unfortunately familiar with—an electroshock machine, a favorite of the Russians, from what I knew. I wasn't looking forward to what would come next.

CHAPTER TWENTY-SEVEN

MARCO

Glass shattered in a violent shower down the wall, amber liquid chasing the shards. I resumed pacing, not feeling the least bit better after throwing the whiskey bottle. *How could this have happened?* It was like a curse, my worst nightmare from when Elena was thought to be dead years ago. Then Sofia had been taken. Both nightmares were brought to life all over again with my wife missing and her guards killed.

The door opened and closed as, one by one, the rest of the bosses to the Five Families joined me with matching expressions of worry and rage. Retribution would be mine.

I swiped my phone from the island but paused when I faced Max, Enzo, and Stefano. We needed to strategize, and I was thinking through a haze of bloodlust. I forced myself to maintain restraint as I filled them in on everything we knew, from finding her guards on the beach to reviewing the video feed and how someone had taken her out of range. The recording hadn't caught anything to indicate who it was. But I knew. It had to have been Yuri. He'd lied about everything.

"We go to him, then." Stefano's icy words penetrated my haze.

"Yes," I agreed. "An unannounced visit." *With deadly intent.*

My soldiers were waiting for my orders. It was time to take action, which I'd been itching to do from the second I felt her absence.

"We'll get her back," Max said as he palmed his Glock.

Enzo and Stefano were armed, their guns in their hands, ready. There was no doubt we would find her and make them pay. I said nothing as I stormed to the elevators, the other bosses on my heels. I would take point. She was my wife.

Before we hit the road at top speed, we loaded our vehicles with weapons to bulldoze our way through the Bratva. I lost time along the drive, images of what could happen to Elena tormenting me. Then we were tearing down the street that led to the mansion. Seconds later, I destroyed the gate across the long driveway with the Hummer I'd decided at the last minute to take.

Bratva soldiers surrounded us as Yuri barged out of the front entrance, yelling orders in Russian. Stefano was at my door, blocking my exit before I could shove it open. "What the hell?"

He glared at me through the window, growling to stand down. *The fuck I will!* I rammed my weight against the door, while Stefano did the same on the opposite side. Max and Enzo took position at the passenger door and in line of the front windshield, effectively blocking any shot I had of the Bratva boss.

"Listen to me," Stefano commanded. "I called ahead. Yuri is expecting us." He leaned down, so we were at the same level. "Don't kill him."

His words penetrated, and I gave a clipped nod. When he backed up, I jumped out then shoved Stefano back. When his enraged eyes met mine, I was ready to throw down, but he wasn't the target.

Yuri was.

Stefano pushed me against the vehicle then leaned in close,

his lips curling back as he growled hushed words through clenched teeth: "He doesn't have her."

Everything in me stilled, and I shoved Stefano back. *If Yuri didn't have El, who the fuck did?* With the new information, Stefano's insistence on a meeting rather than bloodshed made sense. I grunted as I rounded my vehicle, my trigger finger itching to unleash hell on the Bratva. Stefano matched my pace as we strode toward the steps that led to where Yuri and Vic waited.

Enzo, Max, and Stefano flanked me. Yuri and Vic's expressions were grim as we approached. Then Yuri motioned for us to follow them inside. A mix of their soldiers and ours accompanied the six of us as we weaved through rooms until we entered a study that served as Yuri's temporary office. Old tomes lined bookshelves behind the monstrous desk. He rounded the statement piece then stood behind it rather than sitting. None of us had stowed our guns, but we had the decency to order our guards to wait in the hallway with theirs.

Stefano kicked the door shut, giving us the illusion of privacy. I'd had enough silence and ground out the only question that mattered: "Where is my wife?"

"I do not have her," Yuri answered in his thickly accented voice.

"The paternity test was a lie." It made the most sense. The hand at my side that didn't hold a gun clenched into a fist. I watched their every expression, noting the regret and weariness etched on the older Russian's face.

Vic was supposed to be an ally, the brains of the Bratva, but I refused to address him, keeping my focus squarely on the boss.

"When I saw Elena for the first time, it was as if Daniela stood before me." Yuri absently rubbed his whiskers, his gaze far away. "It was such a shock. Then when Vic told me she was my daughter, the pieces fell into place, as did the threat against her." His voice and expression sharpened. "Mischa is missing too."

I didn't care about his wife. *Unless...* "Does she have El?" Mischa stayed in the background. We didn't have a great deal of intel on her.

"My guess is that she has Elena to avenge the death of our son. My wife had an usual bond with Ivan." Yuri briefly glanced at Vic, and a wordless conversation ensued in several seconds before Yuri dropped a horrifying bomb on us. "It's as if she saw herself in him. I've already dispatched men to search for her. She won't have gotten far. Our jets are accounted for and will remain grounded."

It was even worse than I had previously imagined. A grieving mother was unpredictable and capable of vengeful destruction.

<hr>

Elena

When Mischa put on thick, elbow-length rubber gloves, my stomach plummeted. Next, she picked up broad-contact wet electrodes, the kind that wouldn't leave burn marks. The following hour wasn't pleasant. After the first few body-searing, muscle-convulsing shocks, I forced myself to retreat into my mind, to distance myself from the pain until those blissful moments of unconsciousness took over.

When I came to and she'd finished shocking me, I reclined on the table that she'd had her men move into the room. My body felt raw and tenderized from the volts of electricity that had shot through my system. When I wasn't unconscious, I'd spent the minutes between sessions listening to her lament about her son.

I'd never met Ivan, and I was glad. He sounded terrifying, but she was immensely proud of him. With little else to do besides try to get out of the ropes that bound me to the table, I studied her. Mischa was tall and breathtaking—if I didn't look closely and notice the insanity behind her deceptively pretty brown eyes. Her hair was cut at an angle to frame her face, ending just beneath her chin. It worked for her, but there was nothing that could hide the psychosis on full display before me, which chilled my blood to arctic degrees.

She no longer held the electrodes, and I looked around the room as much as I could in anxiety about what would be next. I hoped the tools she'd unraveled upon entry to the room remained out of her hands and far away from me. The too-loud screech of a chair against the cement floor echoed through the enclosed space as Mischa dragged it close then sat down.

My head lolled toward her. *Please let this be the part where she states her evil plan.* I needed a reprieve and to buy time for Marco to find me. They'd knocked me unconscious at the beach, so I didn't know how far we'd gone and didn't have any landmarks to help figure it out.

"I knew your mother." She stated, her eyes devoid of expression. "She captivated my husband, which didn't bother me. I had other things to do, and she took up some of his time. There had been others. But Daniela, she was different. I didn't notice it immediately, not until Yuri spent more time with her, even taking her with him when he went away for business." She looked at her nails then back to me, her features turning hard. "I couldn't let her step fully into my shoes, and from the way he treated her, I could see the inevitability of that happening. I decided it was time for her to go away, have a little accident."

Saliva pooled in my mouth, and I gulped it down, working to maintain my composure while the woman recalled details of planning my mother's death as if she were reading a shopping list.

"Imagine my surprise when I found Daniela in the bathroom, a positive pregnancy test in her hand."

When I didn't react, her sculpted brows rose. She'd already

introduced herself as my stepmother. She was aware I had the same information about my lineage that she did. What I hadn't realized was how long she'd known, but I kept that horrifying little nugget to myself. "But you didn't kill her." I had to keep her talking, even if I didn't want to hear any of it.

"There was a commotion, and I was pulled away, but not before telling her I knew what she was and that if she didn't leave, I would tell my husband all about how she was a spy for the Italians."

"Did you tell Yuri?"

"About Daniela being a spy? Yes. It worked well for me. I sent soldiers after her while my husband drowned himself in vodka."

Yuri did have feelings for my mother, then. "But they failed?"

She chuckled, and I suppressed a shiver at how downright eerie the sound was. "It took them a long time to locate her. Years. I was patient. My boys needed me."

"Did Yuri know Ivan was looking for me?" *Or had she sent him?*

"Not at first." I could tell she was reliving the memories by the distance in her response. "Ivan was too young to be of much help when Daniela left our household. But when he grew into the man I knew he would be, I shared the details of her infiltration and how an enemy born of her body still lived. There had been no proof that the child we tracked had died. Ivan vowed to rectify that."

"He wanted to kill his half sister?" It wasn't a surprise, not if he was like his mother. But I was desperate for anything that would keep her talking.

Her face relaxed. "Ivan was made in my image. I expected great things from him. Vic, although brilliant, is just like his father. Analytical, practical, and allows compassion and misplaced loyalty to cloud his judgment, so much like my husband." She sighed before returning her gaze to mine. "Vic should have died. Not my Ivan."

I tensed beneath my restraints, wishing they were looser so I could fight my way out. I sensed she was nearing an end to her reminiscing. I could see the finality, the determination stamped across her taut features. She planned to kill me soon.

"But I have you. And for these brief moments in time, your pain has called out to Ivan. We are linked, the three of us. I can sense my son. He is close and eager to watch you die."

CHAPTER TWENTY-EIGHT

MARCO

Yuri tracked the phones of the absent soldiers to a warehouse on the south side of the city. Heavy drops of rain plummeted from dark clouds overhead, and gusts of frigid wind rustled torn sheets of newspapers yellowed with age. We stepped with care so as not to disturb cans or glass left by careless pedestrians or homeless people. Rust peppered the structure where the windows met debilitated steel.

As we moved with care toward our target, I ground my teeth, thinking of how Yuri had only given us the information when we agreed to let his wife live. The guards aiding her, however, didn't matter. I'd said what I had for efficiency. Every moment was precarious while El's life hung in the balance.

As for my promise—I had no intention of leaving Mischa alive.

With silencers on our guns for added stealth, we crept along the sides of the warehouse, taking care to remain out of view of the windows. Yuri and Vic were on the opposite side with Stefano, while Max and Enzo went with me. We would meet at the front of the building to overtake the guards before any alarm sounded. Vic had removed the single sniper positioned across the street on the run-down apartment complex's roof. Yuri determined there would be one or two guards at the entrance and another two inside with Mischa.

We rounded the corner at the same time as the other three from our team. Both sides fired shots, and the guards went down with muffled thumps on the cement. Then we were inside.

Dimly lit, the old packaging building appeared devoid of people. Boxes on crates obscured portions of the warehouse. The equipment was sparse but efficiently placed. Just past the center of the main space, there were a few doors in the back and what looked like a hallway leading to additional offices and possibly a restroom. A slight scuff sounded, then a soldier exited the area in question.

He spotted us and managed a partial yell before I embedded a bullet in his forehead. I fired another into his chest. But the damage was done. We raced to the hallway, weapons loaded and ready to fire. They would know we were coming from the noise Mischa's guard made before he died.

If our count was accurate, there were two more guards we had to pass. At the edge of the corridor, a slew of gunfire erupted, barring entry. Yuri and I shoved past the prone man bleeding out on the cement. A flurry of Russian words spilled from his lips as we barreled down on the hulking form of another of his men. I didn't wait for the result of whatever he'd said. Instead, I fired off another two shots: head and chest.

The dead soldier had guarded a door at the end of the corridor. That had to have been where Elena was. I kicked the door, and it flew open, slamming into the back wall. Yuri shouted then knocked my arm, causing my bullet to miss its mark—Mischa's forehead—and clip her in the shoulder. All I registered was that she stood over El, who was strapped to a table, the knife raised above her head already on its descent to plunge into her heart.

The spray of blood then the trail of red down Mischa's dominant arm gave me a sense of satisfaction but not nearly what killing her would have.

Yuri continued to shout at his wife while wrestling with me so that I wouldn't kill her.

El flashed me a weak smile. "Hey, honey."

It threw me off balance for a second. For one, she'd never called me a term of endearment before. And two, she'd relaxed as if she wasn't in danger when we entered the room.

I took in Mischa's stance and stopped fighting Yuri, his words finally penetrating. "You gave your word." His voice was gruff but commanding. "She will not kill my daughter."

"Hey, Marco." El's voice was soft, not like her usual self-assured confidence. "Can you get me out of here?"

I was by her side instantly, wrenching the knife from Mischa's hands, fighting myself not to bury it into her heart. Instead, I got to work on severing El's binds. As soon as she was free and in my arms, I took in the contents of the room and my body shook with rage all over again with the need to make Mischa pay.

Stefano, Enzo, and Max obscured my view of the Russian woman and were oddly silent. But I knew if anything happened, if Mischa made even the slightest move, they would have my back.

It was difficult to contain my rage, but I tried not to squeeze her too tightly as I held her to me.

Yuri approached my side, wariness in his light eyes. He rubbed his hand over his goatee-covered chin before speaking, his words directed to my wife. "I am sorry, Elena. She won't come near you again. This, I promise you."

"Damn right she won't." My fingers itched to put a bullet between Yuri's eyes for the harm inflicted upon El. "Mischa dies. That's the only way to make this right."

Elena

S afe in Marco's embrace, I replayed what Yuri had shouted to Mischa in Russian. The more I heard the language, the more I remembered my mother speaking it to me when I was young, in addition to Italian and English. But Mama had only talked in English, so the rest faded into the back of my mind. I was rusty, but I understood him.

Yuri told Mischa he would not forgive her if she harmed me, that she would lose everything and go back to where he'd found her.

I was intrigued but exhausted and wanted to go home. My body ached. My brain hurt. A shower and yoga pants were calling my name. What I wouldn't have given for our home repairs to be done so I could have Marco hold me in the hot tub. That would have been perfect.

His arms tightened as my legs gave out. I was so tired. A nap first then the shower. I let my eyes drift shut as he lifted me into his arms. His voice vibrated through his chest and into mine as he told one of the others to call Trey to meet us at home. We were moving as I lost the fight to stay awake.

I blinked, panic riding my ascent to consciousness. My fingers curled, digging into a soft blanket I lay on. My gaze darted around, cataloging everything I could see as my heart slammed against my rib cage. An IV was hooked up, feeding fluids into a vein in my hand—Trey had been there. The familiarity of our bedroom in the lakefront city greystone took the edge off my fight-or-flight response, and I focused on slowing my breathing to quell the onset of panic.

A low murmur of voices floated to me from the kitchen. Not even two seconds later, Marco was by my side. He loomed over me, concern pulling his lips into a frown. "I'm so sorry, El."

"I'm okay." I relaxed back onto the bed, offering him a reassuring smile as he detached the almost empty IV. "I just needed to rest." I scrunched my nose at the thought of how badly I wanted a shower. "But maybe—"

"You want a shower."

I tapped the end of my nose, and he grinned then helped me up. I didn't need him to do that, but I wasn't complaining. What I wanted, along with being clean, was for him to come in with me. But the voices I'd heard earlier nudged my mind. "Is someone else here? Is it Trey?"

"No. He did an examination and didn't think there would be any issues. If you need him, he'll come back. He's back at the hospital."

Marco was acting weird. "I'm okay. Who's here if it isn't Trey?"

He pursed his lips, looking downright frightening for a moment. "Yuri. Katya is waiting with our guards. She wants to speak to you after Yuri."

"He's here alone?" I was surprised. I would have thought he'd stayed with Mischa—I didn't like knowing she was free to do whatever she wanted. And I wasn't sure how I felt about Yuri being in my home either. I was fine with Katya. Too bad she didn't come in with Yuri.

I looped my arm around Marco's waist. It did feel like my home. "I'll be out in ten minutes." I reluctantly untangled myself from him so I could get cleaned up in record time. I wanted to spend the evening with Marco and no one else, which meant, sooner rather than later, I had to deal with why Yuri was there.

"You'll be all right?"

The worry in his eyes warmed my heart. "Yeah. I'm good. The nap helped." I ran my hands over my hair then tucked it behind my ears before closing the door while he stood there. No good would come of him joining me in the bathroom. I wouldn't be able to keep my hands off him.

Not even ten minutes later, I emerged from the steam-filled room, dressed casually in soft yoga pants and a long sweater. I was going for comfort and didn't care how I looked. My hair was clean, my face devoid of makeup, fuzzy socks on my feet. My fingers trailed the wall as I left our bedroom and made my way to the kitchen, where I suspected Marco and Yuri were.

I had to pause for a moment when they came into sight, two immensely powerful bosses facing one another, each with a glass of whiskey in hand. Neither looked pleased, but at least they weren't trying to kill each other.

I must have made a noise, because they both turned as I crossed the living room to the stool closest to Marco. He took my hand, helped me into the chair, then crowded me. "Do you want a drink, El?"

Do I? I had to think about it for a moment. "No thanks." I wanted a clear head for the conversation. I turned to Yuri. "How are you going to keep Mischa contained?" Because any mother would have a hard time letting go if she thought someone wronged her child, but an imbalanced mother? There was little chance of her plans to enact revenge ever dying.

Yuri rubbed his hand over his whiskers, something I was coming to recognize as a sign of unease or deep regret.

"I'm deeply sorry for all you suffered at my wife's hands, Elena."

I nodded, wanting to get to the root of the problem: how was he going to keep her away from me. "Thank you. Fair warning: if she comes at me again, I will put a bullet between her eyes."

His lips twitched before he regained control. "Mischa will not come near you. I should have addressed her mental state a long time ago, but it hasn't been an issue until now. I give you my word that she will get the help she needs and live the rest of her life under strict supervision."

"That's wonderful, but it doesn't give me the assurance I need to be okay with her living." She was dangerous. I couldn't see her letting go of her vendetta.

"I understand. Here is my assurance to you." Yuri leaned in, conviction reinforcing his every word. "At the slightest sign of Mischa moving against you, she will lose everything. I will return her to the poverty from where I found her in Norilsk. She despises the place. It's only accessible by air and deep within the Antarctic Circle. To her, it is a fate worse than death, especially since everyone will know of her betrayal. The town, which benefitted from her connection to the Bratva, will suffer, ensuring no one helps her."

I tilted my head back to gauge Marco's reaction as his hand tightened on my hip. *Would Yuri's threat be enough?*

We wrapped things up with Yuri, and then Marco accompanied him in the elevator and to his waiting car. He would be back up with Katya, who apparently wanted to talk to me —*alone*—before they left. I chuckled to myself. Marco was not happy with that. He refused. I said too bad. Then we compromised. He would be present.

It didn't matter that she'd saved my life because none of the guys trusted her. Funny, because the girls did, and if she was Italian or defected to our side, she would have been one of us.

I settled on one of the barstools, glad that it was oversized and had a back. I needed the support, as my body felt tenderized and weak. It didn't take long for the elevator to return and for Marco to emerge with Katya. Next to Marco, she looked tiny, her long white-blond hair in an intricate braid that fell over one shoulder. Her light-blue eyes met mine as she came to stand before me, ignoring my scowling husband, who hovered nearby.

"I came to see that you were okay and to say my apologies for not stopping Mischa before she found you."

"Should I be worried about her?" I knew I should, but I wanted her take on it.

She inclined her head once. "Yes. Always. For now, Yuri will have her on a tight leash. Vic and I are watching her. But there will be a time Yuri's guard is down, or he is away, and if we aren't there to stop her, you'll need to. He won't hold anything against you if she strikes again."

It was good information to know, not that I cared what Yuri thought. If his wife went after me, I would end her. The next time, I would be prepared. Katya's eyes sparkled. She knew what I was thinking.

"If you need something from me, you know how to reach me." Her lips twitched. "You're in a unique position."

She pivoted to leave but my words stopped her. "Seems you are too." She gave me that same singular nod before going to the elevator, without Marco, and calling it up. As she stepped inside, our gazes caught and held, and she winked. She'd helped the Italians more than once, and there would be a time in the future we'd learn why and what she wanted to gain from doing so.

As the doors closed, Marco's arm wrapped around my shoulders, and I felt some of the tension leave his body. In time, everything would be made clear, but for now, I wanted to relax within the comfort of his embrace and forget about what I'd just been through.

CHAPTER TWENTY-NINE

MARCO

Brilliant shades of orange, purple, and red painted the sky, spilling into the choppy waters as the sun dipped below the horizon. I'd ordered the heaters El wanted and had them installed as a surprise. We were on the balcony, defying the dropping fall temperatures a few days after she went missing. We'd spent every moment possible together, since I was reluctant to let her out of my sight.

After so many years, to have El as my wife was a dream I never thought I'd have, and I would do everything in my power to ensure she was happy and safe. El needed her independence, her sanctuary away from the world, and to utilize her unique skills. I'd taken note of the private space she'd had on the roof in New Jersey, her reactions to the outdoor living area in our under-construction house in the suburbs, and how she wanted the balcony accessible even when it was too cold. An oasis was essential, and I would provide that for her.

I looped my arms around her as she rested her back against my chest on the lounge chair we shared on the balcony. A fleece throw draped over her legs, warding off more of the chill. Waves rolled and crashed below while steam swirled from the

White Russian she held. Her narrowed eyes and "don't judge me" as she'd heated her drink had made me laugh.

"So"—El tilted her head so that our gazes met—"what do you make of Yuri's decision to manage Mischa?"

"I don't like it, and he should watch his back."

"Yeah, there's that for sure. I'm not happy about it, either, but I understand him being reluctant to do more. She's the mother of his children."

My arms tightened briefly as a spike of anxiety hit my bloodstream at the thought of anything happening to Elena. "We won't let our guard down. I've talked to Vic about it, and he agreed to keep an eye on his mother for both your and Camila's safety."

"That's got to be hard. I can't imagine how he must feel."

"I'm sure it is." I paused. "There are a couple of things I wanted to talk with you about."

"Oh?" She sipped her drink then set it down, tucking her fingers in with mine.

"The renovation, for starters. I appreciate you heading that up. You can make any changes you want." It was her home, too, and I wanted her to be happy with the design.

She laughed, the sound low and sexy, making me want to hurry our conversation and take her to bed.

"I figured but wanted to say it anyway." I pressed a kiss to the top of her head, my gaze trailing the last remnants of the wine-colored lake as the last sliver of the sun hung in the distance. The expanse of water as far as we could see represented free-dom, something she'd had in New Jersey. I didn't want to clip her wings but rather give her something to accentuate her value. "Your ability to break into the Bratva without detection was impressive. Not that I'm happy about it, but your skills do need to be utilized. You're an asset to your family's security. I thought you might like to assess how I've run things and offer improvement."

El pushed up then resettled so that her arms went around my neck, and she straddled my legs.

I groaned at the contact of having her where I wanted her all along. I shifted her so that she was sideways and cradled against me instead. We would go inside soon, but I knew she wanted to enjoy our time outside and wasn't going to rush her. "So that's a yes?"

"Of course it is." Her grin stretched wide, and her oceanic eyes sparkled.

I pushed her hair behind her ear and trailed my fingers along her neck to rest at the thundering pulse at the base.

She pulled my hand away and clasped it in hers, and her expression turned serious. "We only touched on the Bratva break-in. I know you had major issues about Ivan torturing Sofia because of me, and it was one of the reasons you struggled with trusting me." She worried her lower lip with her teeth for a second before releasing it. "Then I involved her in my plan to slip past the Bratva's security. And yeah, we talked about trust. I apologized, but how are you feeling about what I did?" Her brows furrowed briefly. "I'm not saying I wouldn't do it again. I wanted to check in with you."

"I'm done blaming you for involving my sister in running away from us, Ivan's actions, and anything else, really. There were a lot of outside factors that I refused to consider. The main thing was that I was furious at you for leaving. Even though I knew you weren't mine, I wanted you. Then you left, and I thought you were dead." I squeezed her hand. "It did something to me. I never want to experience that again. So, El, I mean it when I say I want you involved in our security. Because in this life, there will always be a fight at our doorstep."

"I get it, but you said that like you know what's coming. What's going on?"

I hooked my arms under her legs and stood with her in my embrace. I had to tell her, but after that, I was done with the conversation. There were better things to do with our mouths instead of talking. "Max has been running his family and also the Brambilla Family—Lil's. They learned some time ago that she has a half brother."

"Do we know who he is?" Her fingers toyed with the ends of my hair at the base of my neck as I carried her to our bedroom.

"We do. His name is Luc Savino, and he has no idea he's connected to the Mafia, but he's about to." When she opened her mouth to respond, I swallowed her words with a kiss. I was done talking. And by the way she eagerly responded to my kiss, so was she.

CHAPTER THIRTY

ELENA

Marco's grin stretched wide, and I couldn't help but laugh at the mischief that flashed in his green eyes. It was Thursday, almost a full week since Mischa had gotten the jump on me. I had almost fully recovered, things were good, and Marco and I were going to try to get away for a few days.

We planned to board our jet for Italy for a delayed honeymoon in less than an hour, and he hadn't told me where we were going. As we pulled into Mama's neighborhood, I had my answer.

I missed her. Even though we saw each other as much as we could, it wasn't enough. She'd given me space because I was newly married, and she thought that was best. It was ridiculous, though, and I planned to set her straight as soon as Marco and I got back from our trip. I squeezed his hand as we came to a stop. "Thank you."

He leaned over and brushed his lips over mine in a too-short caress. "Let's go, Little Thief. We have a library to check out."

I smacked his shoulder, laughing at the old nickname as I got out of the car. We walked up the steps as Mama flung the door open, and I found myself pulled into her arms. I squeezed her back just as tightly.

"It's so good to see you, Baby Girl." Then she released me and tugged Marco in for a hug. "Come inside." She shook her head, her gaze tracking the fat snowflakes that swirled in the slight breeze. She shivered. "How did this even happen? I feel like it shouldn't be snowing until a month or two from now."

"I know. I can't wait to fly out, even if it's only for a couple of days."

We followed Nicole through the house and to the library, pausing when Marco touched my shoulder and told us he would find us in a little while. Max was in the office, going over some old records of Antonio's, and I assumed my new husband was going to join Max there.

I flashed him a small smile, grateful for the time alone with Mama—something he knew I would want. Goose bumps danced over my arms, and the fine hairs at the back of my neck stood on end in anticipation of what we might find.

"Time moves too fast. I don't like it." A touch of sadness coated Mama's voice.

I didn't like it. Her statement solidified even more that we would have to set regular days during the week to get together —some with just the two of us and others with all the girls, as Mama adored them.

Books lined the floor-to-ceiling shelves, and comfortable captain's chairs with blankets thrown over the backs and matching ottomans were grouped in several areas. The room was large but cozy and inviting at the same time.

Mama went toward one of the freestanding bookshelves that contained a variety of genres, including cozy mysteries and romance, a bookcase I grew familiar with in my teen years. The only novels I hadn't read were the *Star Wars* hardcovers that lined the top.

When we'd had breakfast soon after I'd returned home, she'd hinted to visit the library. We'd been interrupted by Max and Tony, and she'd never finished telling me what had seemed important. But I knew there was something else in the there I needed to see.

When she grasped the edge of the bookcase and went up on her toes to pull down one of the *Star Wars* books, I moved to help. I had an inch of height on her petite frame. Once the book was down, she motioned for me to bring it over to our favorite spot, where two buttery-soft leather chairs were arranged before a gas fireplace. There was a small table between the chairs, perfect to rest a few books and a drink. My finger traced the multiple rings I'd made with mugs of hot chocolate when I was younger. Mama had never said a word about the damage to the table.

"I came across this book almost by accident. I was looking for something to read when a random memory about a time Daniela and I were talking popped in my head." She smoothed her hand over the cover. "She and I were discussing how Antonio wanted me to get work done, so I remained forever young and the perfect trophy wife. I was upset about it, and Daniela was always a sympathetic ear. She understood being used. We had that in common." She set her glass down with force, and I worried it would break on impact.

When it didn't, I jerked my gaze to hers in time to witness the shrewdness that lurked beneath the pretty packaging Antonio had obsessed over while failing to note her intelligence. Mama shoved her blond hair back, and a flash of pain pulled the corners of her lips down. "Daniela replaced this book on the shelf, saying they should never underestimate us. Sometimes, what's hidden on the inside is more powerful than the packaging."

I frowned. "I don't remember much about her feeling bad.

But I do remember how Antonio used to treat you. It was another reason why I didn't like him, even though he took me in after my mother died."

Mama relaxed in her chair and crossed her legs. "I don't think Daniela was unhappy. She had you, after all." A spark of warmth lit her eyes, and she seemed to shake off a little of the weighty past.

"Even though Daniela was born into the Mafia, she was a distant cousin and didn't have the same financial privilege as we do. She was happy where she was before Frank found her. Our initiation into this life was very different, but we both came from more humble beginnings." Her gaze sharpened as it locked on to mine. "They always underestimated us, not looking beneath the pretty package they fixated on."

I shivered from the intensity of her words. There was a reason Mama had so many secrets. She was wicked smart and knew that secrets were as good, if not better than, currency.

She sighed and flipped to the beginning of the book, where a single sheet of paper was tucked between the pages. "A different keycode is needed for this message, and I don't know what it is. But something tells me she gave it to you when you were little." She lifted the paper and passed it to me. "It's a note from your mother to you, Baby Girl."

I barely noticed as Mama unfolded herself from the chair. Then she placed a notepad and pen in front of me before squeezing my shoulder. "Come find me when you're done. I'll be in the three-season room."

I nodded as I stared at my mother's loopy script. I let myself remember her most intense moments, when she deviated from her fun and easygoing demeanor. She'd made me practice those drills over and over again, which ultimately saved my life. But another memory hit me, too, of Daughtry's "Over You," a song we would play and sing together.

I closed my eyes and imagined the song, focusing on the

chorus. She told me to use the song as a key, using the number of letters in each of the words in the verse. It was random and brilliant at the same time. Without wasting another second, I transcribed the verse and counted each word, noting the numbers beneath them. Then I went through the note and pulled the corresponding letters until I had what she'd hidden for me to find.

Elena,

I loved you from the moment I learned I was carrying you. Never forget that. You are my world, and I would do anything for you. This is why I taught you everything I thought you would need to survive: how to hide, how to steal, how to be invisible like a ghost, and how to fight. I don't know if I could impart all those skills to the level I planned. My time was ticking. They would find me. I did the best I could to prepare you. I hope it was enough.

When Frank Rossi approached me to work for him, there was no other option other than accepting. I was a spy, and I'd infiltrated the Pavlov Bratva. But things didn't turn out as I thought they would.

The day I met Nicole Caruso felt like fate. Antonio, her husband, had already bribed me to be a double agent of sorts and report on Frank Rossi to him. They were both evil men. I had no allegiance to one over the other, even though I am a distant cousin to Frank. That's something I hid as much as I could. There was no way I wanted you to end up with him if I died. I didn't trust Frank not to hand you over to the Bratva or harm you himself. Nicole was the perfect answer. She loved you from the moment she met you, and I knew she would protect you.

That's one lie I told. There is another. I told you and Nicole that your father was a soldier who died helping me escape, that he was Italian and connected to the Five Families. I didn't reveal a name but gave enough information not to be questioned further. It wasn't true. While working within the Bratva, I grew close to Yuri Pavlov. We fell in love. I never expected that to happen.

I found out I was pregnant with you when Mischa discovered me in the bathroom, holding the test in hand. She is dangerous and why I ran without talking to Yuri, without telling him about you. It was a small miracle that I escaped. I used the Caruso name to further muddy my trail, to hide you. But they already knew about my connection to Frank Rossi.

You are in a position where your blood straddles powerful Mafia families. While the choice where you are most comfortable will always be yours, know that you are accepted and tied to the Italian-American Mafia through me. Never question who you are—I raised you as an Italian, and if I'm correct and my days are limited, Nicole will take you in to her family. You are a Mafia princess. It's who you are meant to be.

I've done my best to hide you, to lay false trails, but if Mischa finds you, go to Yuri. All he'll need to see is your face, your eyes, and he will connect the timing with when I left to you—and see the possibility that you're his child.

I'm so proud of you. Be safe, my daughter.

I love you,

Daniela

Tears rolled down my face as I sat there, my mother's words sinking in, resonating. If only I had found the note before I'd left... I wondered if I would have done things differently, if I would have left at all, feeling even more displaced than I instinctually did while growing up.

I pushed out a breath and wiped my face dry. My pity party needed to end. I gathered the papers and returned the *Star Wars* book, chuckling as I realized my mother had a dark sense of humor to hide the note in there, as it was the volume where Luke learned who his father was. I knew Mama would find the humor in it too. It was time I found her and shared what my mother had written.

The three-season room, Mama's and my second-favorite place in the house, was at the back. I moved through the newly decorated and lighter rooms until I found her sitting on the love seat amid lush plants. Marco and Max were there, keeping her company.

Three sets of concerned eyes met mine as I entered the tropical oasis Mama had created. I waved away their worry, sat beside Mama, and filled them in on what I'd learned from my mother's letter.

"Well"—a mischievous smile curved Mama's mouth—"interesting choice of books."

"Right?" I laughed, and the guys joined us.

The letter was something I'd needed, and I'd probably found it at exactly the right time. I was happy with my choices and where I'd ended up, and if I'd known too much too soon, I wasn't sure what my future would have held.

I turned to Marco, my eyebrows raised. He knew what I wanted to know—more about the honeymoon we'd planned on taking. We needed to leave in the next few minutes.

From what I'd learned from my friends and my initiation back home, the Bratva attacks behind us, it was clear we had one battle after another ahead of us. The next one was headed our way. I acknowledged the possibility that whatever happened next could go smoothly, but that wasn't the Mafia way.

"We're good. Max anticipates being home after the weekend with Luc."

I had to wonder if Lil was nervous about meeting her half brother. I turned to Max. "Do you think Luc will assume his role seamlessly?"

Max chuckled. "Hell no. It's going to be a shit show. But we need someone strong to run the Brambilla family, and I can't run it and mine forever."

"From what little I know about Luc, he should have what it takes," Marco added.

"That brings up the part about where he'll go once we return to Chicago." Max looked pointedly at Mama. "Lil doesn't want us to stay in her old home with Luc while we groom him to take over. What would you think about us crashing here with you and Tony?"

Mama laughed, her expression sharpening. "In other words, you want me to keep an eye on things and see what I can uncover?"

"Yes," Max said simply.

"Sure, honey. I've got no problems with it. The more, the merrier."

"You say that now…" Max shook his head.

"It'll be fun having my daughter-in-law around. Don't you worry about a thing."

"And on that note"—Marco stood and reached for my hand—"we have a flight to catch."

Mama jumped to her feet and wrapped her arms around me. "You have a wonderful time, Baby Girl." When she pulled back, tears misted her eyes. "I love you, El."

"I love you, too, Mama." I pressed a kiss to her cheek then let Marco tug me toward the door. "Later, Max!"

"Have fun, you two." Max grinned before sitting back down and leaning toward Mama. They were probably going to plan how to handle initiating a new boss, a man who knew nothing about his heritage, into the family.

We left them to their discussion and headed for the door.

After Marco opened the car door for me then went around and got into his seat, I grinned. "I can't wait to get out of here with you to enjoy a few days of peace while we can."

He put the car in gear, and we sped down the driveway and toward the airport, where our jet waited. In no time, we were at the airport, through security, and aboard our private plane. We taxied down the runway then lifted off, but I let a few more minutes pass before the pressure of the day eased from my shoulders.

We'd opted for seats side by side instead of across from each other and with a table between us on the other side of the aisle. My fingers threaded with his. I needed to touch him.

"I'm sorry we can't take more time for our honeymoon. I want to spend a month with you in Italy." Marco lifted my hand and pressed a kiss to it.

We were going to our other home in Italy, one I had yet to see. But he'd described the beautiful sea view from the back of the home, complete with an outdoor kitchen and a heated infinity pool that gave the impression of feeding into the sea. I couldn't wait to escape the cold weather in Chicago and have Marco all to myself.

"I'll take any time I can get where it's just the two of us." I moved closer and snuggled against his solid frame. He lifted his arm and tucked me against his side. Then I smoothed back the thick strands of black hair that had fallen over his forehead, taking any excuse to touch him. "Besides, it's what we do with these few days that'll make our small escape hold us over until the next time we can get away."

"Do you have any idea how much I love you, El?"

His deep voice sent a jolt of longing through me. "Yes." He showed me all the time. "As much as I love you." It didn't matter where we were or what adventure we were on, so long as we were together. I'd never thought my life would turn out the way it had, and I wouldn't change a thing, as long as I got to spend it with the man I'd always wanted.

The End

Continue reading the Mafia Elite series with RUTHLESS HEIR.

https://amymckinleyauthor.com/mafia-elite/

If you enjoyed reading SAVAGE SECRETS as much as I did writing it, I hope you'll consider leaving a review.

RUTHLESS HEIR

RELEASING MARCH 2022

A Mafia crown to claim ...

The crown had always been Luc Savino's. He just didn't know it until a Chicago Mafia boss persuades him to board a jet and assume his destiny. But he won't go without Summer—a one-night stand, his new, secretive executive assistant and probable spy for the former CEO of his latest hostile takeover.

She can only run so far before they find her...

After a mob boss viciously attacks Summer Johansson in her apartment, she flees the state to hide. But when she learns of her best friend's murder and finds herself in the arms of a handsome stranger, her troubles escalate as she's dragged into the heart of the very world she's running from.

Secrets have the power to destroy, but hers will bring them closer...

Summer isn't telling him everything, but Luc finds her impossible to resist. As their trust in one another grows, Summer's enemies close in. Despite all the lies between them, it's the truth that could tear them apart.

Continue reading the Mafia Elite series with RUTHLESS HEIR.

https://amymckinleyauthor.com/mafia-elite/

ACKNOWLEDGMENTS

Mafia Elite has been so much fun. I'm enjoying these books so much, and I hope you are too!

I have a fantastic group of people to thank for being there, from start to finish, of Savage Secret's creation. I am fortunate to have these incredible women—authors—share their input, support, and encouragement. Emily Albright, Kristin Kisska, and Candace Irvin. My editors, Kate Birdsall and Taylor Anhalt, helped shape this story into what it is today. I'm very grateful for the support from my husband and our four kids.

Thank you to T.E. Black Designs, who always exceeds my expectations. Colleen Noyes with Itsy Bitsy Book Bits, and Danielle Sanchez with Wildfire Marketing Solutions, are outstanding. I'm lucky to have them in my corner, working their magic to make each release a success.

Last but certainly not least, a special thank you to all the bloggers and readers who have encouraged and helped me along the way and who continue to make my dream a reality.

Thank you.

ABOUT THE AUTHOR

 Amy McKinley is the *USA Today* best-selling author of the romantic suspense thriller Gray Ghost Novels, Deadly Isles Special Ops, Covert Recruits, Mafia Elite, Moonlit Destination Series, the Five Fates paranormal romance books, and several standalone titles. Her edge-of-your-seat books are filled with surprising twists and just the right amount of heat and danger. She lives in Illinois with her husband, two daughters, two sons, and three mischievous cats.

You can find her at: www.AmyMcKinley.com

Subscribe to Amy's newsletter for book announcements: http://eepurl.com/dEBqJn

goodreads.com/amymckinley_author
bookbub.com/authors/amy-mckinley
facebook.com/amymckinleyauthor
instagram.com/amymckinleyauthor

Irina

Sasha

Zena

Nadia

Katya

-

Standalone Titles

Shattered Melody

Siren's Call: Cursed Seas

Fake Fiancé (A Second Chance Office Romance)

-

Moonlit Destination Series

Moonlit Whisper

Moonlit Kiss

Moonlit Mirage

Five Fates Series

Hidden

Taken

www.ingramcontent.com/pod-product-compliance
Lightning Source LLC
Chambersburg PA
CBHW070944190726
48292CB00004B/1329